ADVANCE SOUTH!

An expedition is digging at Lukka Oasis in search of a lost civilisation. But when valuable gold coins are uncovered, the men are massacred by their Arab bearers, and only a woman escapes. When a party of three legionnaires decides to desert from Post D, each has his own good reason for doing so. Their first destination: Lukka Oasis. But in escaping from the Legion post, they inadvertently set fire to it. What follows is a fight for survival in the desert, with danger and death stalking all parties involved . . .

JOHN ROBB

ADVANCE SOUTH!

Complete and Unabridged

LINFORD
Leicester

First published in Great Britain

First Linford Edition
published 2019

A catalogue record for this book is available
from the British Library.

ISBN 978–1–4448–4269–2

1

The Oasis

They were without mercy. Without fear. They butchered four out of the five members of the Kansas Archaeological Society's North African Expedition. But they did not kill for pleasure. They did so for the most compelling reason known to the mind of man — for money.

The expedition had been at Lukka Oasis for five days. They were highly satisfied with their excavations. The twenty Dylak Arabs, hired far back at Reggan, were proving able and willing workers. They wielded their spades with intelligence. Already two sandstone walls had been uncovered. Also a peculiar building (probably dating back to the fifteenth century), which may have been a merchant's counting house. Or even a shrine at which offerings were made. At all events, they had found several hundred coins there.

Dr. Rufus Westlake, a Harvard graduate and leader of the expedition, sat alone at a trestle table in his tent examining the coins. They had just been washed in the dank oasis water.

They were fascinating . . .

Most of them were of gold and clearly of ancient Levant origin. Which bore out his theory that this remote and untenanted Algerian oasis was once a resting-place on a great overland trade route from Syria to the North-West African coast. Other coins — crudely minted in soft unalloyed silver — were certainly the currency of the Saracens.

Carefully, Dr. Westlake listed them in a leather notebook. He was a careful man, not given to guesswork. Where he was not certain of the correct description of a coin, he prefaced his annotation with a large query mark.

He was glad when he had finished the work. He piled the assortment of precious metal into a small wooden case and locked the lid. Then he stood at the entrance to the tent.

Almost sunset.

Dr. Westlake peered a trifle short-sightedly across the red sand, which seemed redder than ever just now. Then at the small group of wizened palms which sprouted near the artesian well. They were very still, those palms. Not a whisper of air to sway them. He wondered if there was going to be a sandstorm. He recalled hearing that such storms were usually preceded by a strange quiet.

Sweat on his face caused his spectacles to steam over. They often did that in this climate. He wished he had remembered to buy a de-misting preparation while he was at Reggan — the last remnant of civilisation in the area.

When he replaced the polished lenses, he blinked round again.

To his right were the three tents of the other archaeologists.

To the left, and set slightly further apart, was Ruth's tent. The flap was open. He could just discern her slim form, like a silhouette, as she lay resting on the camp bed.

I was worried about bringing her, he thought. *But that was foolish of me. I think she's quite enjoying it all. It must be an interesting experience for her. I only hope she doesn't get bored . . .*

His daughter faded out of his mind as he concentrated on the scene of the diggings.

He saw the ugly heaps of sand and rock which marked the site of the uncovered stonework. It did not look much, that stonework. But to archaeologists, it was of extraordinary significance . . .

Dr. Westlake knew that his three colleagues would be there now, standing seven feet below ground level, supervising the toiling Dylaks. He decided to join them.

It was a sixty-yard walk to the excavation site. As he strolled towards it, Dr. Westlake murmured to himself: 'It certainly is very quiet.'

When he had covered a third of the distance, he stopped.

He did not know precisely why he did so. Not at first. Then he realised that a familiar sound was absent. A sound which

4

should have been clearly audible.

There was no clang of spades. No sound from the Arabs.

'Odd,' he said. 'Very odd. And it's not time for them to finish work . . . '

He hurried on.

Dr. Westlake stopped again when he was almost at the edge of the long ditch. He could see the bottom of it.

And he saw his colleagues — Professor Tarle, Professor Stein and Mr. Batchford. They lay at the southern end of the ditch. At first, Dr. Westlake had a confused notion that they were resting. They looked so very peaceful.

Then he saw the flies. Repulsive flies. They were concentrated in three distinct and faintly humming masses round the inert men. Humming round the blood which oozed through their thin shirts.

He blinked frantically round for the Dylaks. They were in the centre of the ditch, pressed against the far parapet. All twenty of them. Staring at him. Each of them had a completely unblinking stare which made their dark eyes seem vaguely artificial. And each of them held an unsheathed knife. They were short, cruel knives. Slightly curved, like attenuated scimitars. The blades of some of them were stained a light shade of red.

It was only when they began to climb out of the ditch to move towards him that Dr. Westlake fully appreciated what had happened. And why.

For a few moments he was paralysed. Not through fright. He was no coward. But because of sheer horror. The realisation that the Dylak Arabs, who were being well paid, could do this to gain the ancient coins numbed his mind. Yet at the same time, he recalled hearing that one had to be careful of the Dylaks . . .

The nearest of the Arabs was less than three yards from him when he turned and ran. He had remembered Ruth.

There was a revolver somewhere in his tent. He had felt rather foolish about bringing it with him. And he was not altogether certain how to use it. But if he could get his hands on it, he might frighten the Arabs off. Then his daughter, at least, might get away.

In his young days at Harvard, a good

thirty years ago, Dr. Westlake had been a noted runner. In desperation, some of his early ability returned to him. He heard the sandalled feet pounding behind him. Very close. But they were not gaining. Neither was he.

Then he knew that even if he maintained the lead, he would not have time to grope around for the gun. The Dylaks would be on him in a moment. And Ruth would be left defenceless. Ruth was sleeping in her tent. She did not know . . .

Instinctively, he changed course slightly towards her tent. He realised that a strong wind was now blowing across his face. Bits of sand were stinging against his skin. A sandstorm was coming fast. In a few minutes there would be no visibility. She might get away.

He sucked in a retching breath. 'Ruth!'

It was all he could manage. A quivering scream which mingled with the gathering wind. But it was loud enough. Through the haze of swirling sand, he saw his child for the last time.

She stood under the open tent flap.

Tall, fair, lovely. Just like her mother had been. Hands on her slim hips, which were clad in cord riding breeches.

He saw her start to move towards him. Saw the baffled terror in her face. He screamed again.

'Don't, Ruth! Leave me . . . you can't do anything!'

The effort of shouting the two disconnected sentences was too much. Involuntarily, it had slowed his running. A hand was on his shoulder, pulling him back. He pulled it away and stumbled on. But another hand took its place. Then two bare brown arms circled his waist.

His pince-nez spectacles were knocked off. They hung loose on their cord. For some ridiculous reason, he fumbled for them. But he never found them. And for that reason, he did not clearly see the wicked blades which slashed towards his body.

★   ★   ★

She ran towards her father. But suddenly he was lost to sight behind a thick haze of driven sand. For a moment that haze thinned, and she glimpsed a group of shaded figures. Contorted and unnatural figures, like men dancing a lewd ballet. Somewhere, he was among them. But when she reached the spot, there was nothing. Nothing but the wind and the lashing, concealing dimness. She ran blindly on, hell in her heart.

2

Nerves

All that day, Lieutenant Anton Garnia had felt uneasy. He did not know why.

Now it was evening, and his nerves were stretched tighter than ever. He was tempted to indulge in the ridiculous to gain relief. Tempted, for example, to lock himself in his cupboard of an administrative office and sing at the top of his voice. Or to take a running kick at the ridiculous little walls which enclosed Post D.

He stood taut in the compound, like a coiled spring. He flicked his cane. Irritable flicks, without a target. His large, slightly effeminate eyes were confused.

Garnia told himself: *I wear the uniform of a soldier, but I have the soul of a poet. I am sensitive to atmosphere. I know there is something wrong in this awful place. Sacre! If only I could know what it is!*

He had been standing near the door to the men's mess room. He was reminded of the fact when Corporal Jurgan, a Dutchman, emerged after making the evening inspection. There was something reassuring about Jurgan. He was a cheerful, well-nourished-looking N.C.O. Imperturbable, too. In many ways, the opposite of his commanding lieutenant.

Jurgan saluted happily, a smile on his rotund face. As he returned the courtesy, Garnia came to a decision. He would confide in his senior N.C.O.

After all, he thought, he was in an unenviable position. The command of a tiny and lonely Legion post such as his was one of the most unpopular of tasks. He was the only officer in a miniature garrison of thirty-two men. For a three-month tour of duty, they lived together in this preposterous stone box. But the others could talk freely with each other. They could grumble and curse. He, Lieutenant Garnia, was isolated from them even as he lived among them. He alone had a separate room in which he attended to the routine paperwork, ate and slept. It was an unnatural segregation, even though it was necessary.

Perhaps that was what was reacting on his nerves . . . Making them feel like plucked violin strings . . . making the muscles in the depth of his belly contract into a solid ball.

He said to Corporal Jurgan: 'Is everything all right?'

For a fraction of a moment, Jurgan seemed to hesitate. His normal smile faded slightly. '*Oui, mon officier.*'

'You know, corporal, I've had a strange feeling all day.'

He paused deliberately. Jurgan regarded him with respectful interest.

'I've had the feeling that all is not as it should be. That is all. A sort of sixth sense. But I cannot think of any reason for it. Can you?'

Corporal Jurgan shook his head, reflecting a nice blend of polite concern and formal reassurance.

'No, *mon officier.*'

'The men are all right, aren't they?'

'But certainly! They get bored, of course . . . They snarl one at another.

They complain of the food. They complain of you and of me. But that does not mean anything. I think they are very happy.'

Jurgan's main shortcoming was that he could not conceive of anyone being less satisfied with life than he. And Jurgan was one of those fortunates who is perpetually pleased with almost everything.

With his cane, Garnia made a sweeping and emphatic gesture. It reflected his high proportion of Italian blood. Garnia came from Monaco, on the south-east coast of France, where there is little detectable difference between the two nationalities.

He complained: 'But I am very perceptive, corporal. I sense things that other people miss — you understand?'

Jurgan nodded merrily. 'Certainly, *mon officier*. I understand very well.'

But it was clear that he did not. Garnia changed his tone, realising suddenly that he was making himself appear foolish.

'But it doesn't matter, corporal. Forget about it. Carry on . . . '

They again exchanged salutes. Corporal Jurgan, slightly puzzled, continued his rotund progress toward guardroom.

And Garnia went to his office. He locked the door. He flung his kepi on a bunk, which filled nearly half the available space. Then he sang. He did not sing as he wanted to in order to give his nerves full relief. Not at the top of his voice. In fact, the sound he produced scarcely more than a discreet hum. But it helped.

When his song was finished, he swung a leg and aimed a vicious kick at the wall. It almost dislocated his ankle. He felt much better.

★   ★   ★

Three legionnaires sat on an empty bunk. They were staring at a rough sketch map. Their half-naked bodies concealed the map from the others in the mess room. But the precaution was not necessary. Most of the others were sleeping or playing cards at the far end of the room.

The three spoke in urgent whispers, in the manner of men who are not familiar with the art of secrecy but are compelled to practise it.

14

Katz said: 'Danger? I tell you there is none . . .'

He was a German, this Katz. Bred in the Prussian district of Wurttemberg. He exuded gross power, as a bull exudes power. It flowed with the sweat from each pore of his great and hairy torso. It was there in his large, dark, flat face too. The uncompromising vigour of the basic beast. And dangerous because it had a sensual personality allied to a shrewd brain.

Katz continued after a heavy pause: 'Listen to me! Nothing can stop us if we are determined. After we have got over the first fifty-five kilometres, it will be child's play. You, my American friend, make difficulties. You talk of danger when you mean hardship. *Ach!* What is hardship? Nothing. I tell you! Nothing when the reward is freedom!'

He fixed a glare at Legionnaire Eddie Hayle. The American was unmoved by the hostility. He scratched his fair head.

Hayle said smoothly: 'All the same, fifty-five kilometres is a lot of ground to cover. And even if we make it, we might wait weeks before an Arab caravan comes along.'

'*Nein!* Look again at this map I have drawn for you. It is a good map. I know the place. There is the Lukka Oasis. Once we get there, we are as good as free. We will take supplies, so we will be able to wait in comfort for the caravan into Spanish Sahara. When it comes . . . we join it. After that, we go to the port of Villa Cisneros to find a good ship.'

They bent once more over the pencilled map, although it was already familiar.

Hayle still looked doubtful. He, too, was a big man. Not big in the ox-like sense of the German, but taller; swifter. He suggested the flowing rhythm of an athlete.

'Lieutenant Garnia's no fool,' Hayle said. 'Maybe he's a bit excitable, but he knows his job. He'll know the only possible place for us to make for is the Lukka Oasis.'

Katz snorted. 'It does not matter. Let him send out a search squad for us! If he does, we will move away until they have gone — and that will not be long. He cannot afford to play hide and seek with us. There are few enough men here. Is that not so, Boroff?'

The third man nodded eagerly. Legionnaire Boroff was always eager to agree with Katz; he was afraid of the German. All his life he had been afraid of something. His childhood had been spent in Paris where his White Russian parents were refugees of the Red Revolution. Then he had feared the drunken furies of his broken and dissolute father. Later he had feared poverty. Now it was Katz.

'Yes,' Boroff bleated, 'we will be safe. Your plan is good.'

Hayle glanced through the small windows. The sun was almost down and the wind was gathering. Katz followed his gaze.

'This is our opportunity,' Katz hissed. 'Look! Soon there will be a sandstorm. That and the darkness will make it easy for us. We will be gone and no one will see us go. Not even one shot will be fired at us.'

Hayle nodded. The point was obviously

true. The low walls of Post D did not in themselves offer much obstacle to men who wished to desert. And under cover of the gathering storm, a desertion would be doubly easy — anyway, in its opening phases. But another difficulty occurred to him.

'We could lose our direction in the storm,' he said. 'And there's a hell of a lot of desert to wander about in.'

Katz tapped the hip pocket of his slacks. 'I have a compass. I know the bearings.'

For a few moments they became silent. They listened to the gathering whine of the wind. To the patter of driven sand against the walls.

Katz twisted round on the bunk. He put one huge hand on Hayle's shoulder, the other on Boroff's. He looked hard at them. 'We all *want* to get out of here, do we not?'

Boroff nodded immediately. Hayle followed after a pause. Katz smiled, showing broken teeth and emitting foul breath.

'And we all have good reason for

wishing to say farewell to the Legion — but to each of us, that is his own private business. Now I tell you this is our opportunity. In an hour it will be dark and the storm at its height. You know the plan . . . '

Yes, they knew the plan well enough. In its opening stages, it depended on Boroff. For Boroff had been chosen to steal the food supplies. That slightly built little fellow could move like a shadow . . .

★   ★   ★

There was little about Post D to distinguish it from other tiny tactical bases in North Africa — except, perhaps, that it was more remote than most.

It was a miniature fort; a dwarfed and feeble parody of the real thing. The entire structure was scaled down to a quarter of full size.

The square outer walls were a mere nine feet high. In a real fort, they rose to nearly forty feet. Their length was only a trifle over twenty yards — compared to a hundred yards. The garrison strength was thirty-two men and a lieutenant. Just twenty-five percent of fort strength.

In short, Post D was not primarily intended as a defensive base. It had not been built to withstand serious assault. It was no more than a form of permanent encampment where legionnaires lived while keeping law and order in the sub-command area.

That a handful of soldiers were expected to keep the peace in an area of two thousand square miles was accepted as normal, both by the legionnaires and the nomadic Arab populations. The post was more than a centre from which force was available to deal with disorder. It was also a place to which Arabs could go to argue civil disputes before the commanding lieutenant. And the lieutenant's verdicts on such important matters as the disputed ownership of a goat or camel were usually accepted with good grace by the Arabs. Which said much for the status which the Legion enjoyed in Morocco and Algeria.

Post D compound building was a single block of red sandstone, rising rather higher than the surrounding outer walls. A small open space surrounded it. The men's mess, where they both ate and slept, was at the north end. The kitchen adjoined the mess. Then followed the commanding lieutenant's room, in which was contained the Post's radio equipment. Finally, there was the magazine. Here were stored two dozen spare Lebel rifles, three hundred hand-grenades, and ten thousand rounds of .300 small arms ammunition. Normally, the magazine would have been sunk below ground, or detached from the rest of the building. But at Post D, space did not permit of such safety measures.

★　★　★

It was nine o'clock in the evening, when the storm had reached a lashing intensity, that Legionnaire Boroff prepared to steal the food which is a necessity for deserters.

Boroff, of course, was afraid.

He was afraid of what would happen if he failed. He was afraid of what fate had in store if he succeeded. But most of all, he was afraid of Katz, who had deputed him for the task.

He quivered slightly as he pulled on his uniform. He fumbled with his *bougeron*. He almost tied himself in knots as he wound his *ceinture* sash around his waist.

Katz watched him with glowering contempt. 'Hurry! Are you such a fool that you've forgotten how to dress yourself?'

Boroff smiled weakly. Then he glanced anxiously at the other bunks. They showed only dimly under the roof lamp.

Hayle felt sorry for the wretched Russian. He tried to reassure him. 'You don't need to worry. They're sleeping and they haven't noticed anything.'

Boroff's lips quivered. 'The guard changes in two hours . . . they'll all be awake by then!'

Katz mumbled an obscene oath. 'Stupid swine! In two hours we'll be a long way from here . . . do you understand what you must do?'

Boroff nodded wildly. It was perfectly clear, even to his fuddled brain. He knew that no one would be in the kitchen at this time. Indeed, the cook-corporal who ministered there could at this moment be seen dozing on his bunk. He was to take three valises with him when he entered the kitchen. He was to force open the store cupboard with his bayonet. He was to fill each valise with dried food — pemmican biscuits, goat's meat and the like. Then he was to leave the kitchen by the outer door, where the two others would be waiting.

Full equipment was necessary for the escape. Therefore, Boroff, like Hayle and Katz, would be heavily laden.

Hayle and Katz were already fully dressed. Ammunition pouches containing one hundred and twenty rounds were over their greatcoats. They waited impatiently for Boroff.

He was ready at last. Three empty valises hung over his arm. His Lebel was slung across his back. Sweat oozed down his thin and comparatively pale face.

Katz jabbed him with a forefinger. 'The kitchen'll be in darkness,' he said. 'Don't try to light the lamp. And if anyone comes in — hide. You're small and you'll find it easy. Now move!'

Boroff moved unhappily towards the kitchen door. He opened it cautiously, aware of two pairs of eyes watching him. He allowed himself only a narrow aperture, slipped through, and closed the door behind him.

The darkness was absolute. For a few moments he stood very still, trying to visualise the geography of the place. He recollected that a large old stove was on his left. Beyond that, a steel water tank. The store cupboard — a large wooden structure — was set against the wall opposite the stove. It would be locked, most likely. But even Boroff did not anticipate much difficulty in forcing it.

He groped forward. The foresight of his rifle caught against an iron pan suspended from a hook. But the clanging sound was almost entirely drowned by the storm. Suddenly he realised that he did not need to be especially quiet; that storm would cover any ordinary noise he was likely to make.

As he shuffled on, he pressed the empty canvas valises against his chest, while his free left hand was extended. That hand contacted the cupboard. He knew it was the cupboard by the feel of the thing. At the same moment, his boot hit a hard object on the floor. He heard it turn over and apparently roll away. Boroff wondered what it was. He decided that most likely it was a pad of waste. It was not worth bothering about.

His fingers located a crevice at the join between the cupboard's double doors. Swiftly (and like most nervous men, Boroff could move with extraordinary speed) he drew his bayonet. Using his fingers as a guide, he inserted the blade in the space, which was immediately below the lock. He pressed sideways, employing full leverage. Faintly, he heard the wood creak. This was followed by a more pronounced sound as screws parted from their lodgements. And the store cupboard doors swung open in his face.

Now a miscellany of odours smote his nostrils. The musty dryness of semi-stale flour which he knew reposed in sacks at the bottom. The tang of salt in wooden boxes. The heavy fragrance of coffee. He thought, too, that he could identify the smell of biscuits and dried meat.

Biscuits and dried meat . . .

That was what he wanted.

But where were they? How could he place his hands on them in this absolute blackness?

Katz had said: 'Don't try to light the lamp.'

It had been easy for Katz to say that. But Katz had not realised how impossible it was going to be to find what was needed under such conditions.

There was only one answer. He must strike a match. Just for a moment. Katz could not possibly object to that. It was not the same as lighting the roof lamp. No one would see.

After fumbling, Boroff re-inserted his bayonet in its scabbard. Then he found a box of matches in his *capote* pocket. He struck one. In the brief and blinding light, he got a clear picture of the cupboard's contents. At head level he saw piles of long white strips. That was dried goat meat. On the shelf above there were canvas sacks. These, he knew, held biscuits.

He blew out the match. Working from memory, he began to fill the three valises. The meat went in first. That was easy. But when he drew a biscuit sack towards him, he found that it was tied with a stout cord at the neck. He had to use his bayonet for a second time, to cut it.

But in ten minutes he was finished. The three valises were filled. He tested their weight. It was formidable. Now all that remained was to slip through the outer door into the compound, where Katz and Hayle would be waiting.

A ridiculous doubt occurred to Boroff. Were they biscuits that he had been packing? He had not actually seen them . . . he had relied on his familiarity with their packing. But suppose the sack had contained something else! Soap, for example . . .

He quailed with horror at the prospect. Katz would surely kill him.

Boroff decided that he must be sure on the point. He produced another match. Bending down, he struck it and examined the valises. No need to worry. They were biscuits all right. He tossed the match aside and picked up his burden.

Boroff was breathing fast when he reached the outer door. He had unpleasant visions of the corporal-cook suddenly appearing. He slobbered a prayer for divine protection as he pulled back the bolts.

Then suddenly the door blew open under the fury of the wind. He staggered out, half closing his eyes against pellets of sand.

Two dim figures moved towards him. They took two of the valises from him.

He heard Hayle say: 'You've done mighty well, Boroff. Now to get over that wall and out of here . . . '

* * *

The last match which Boroff had lit glowed faintly on the stone floor. It was no longer burning. It was no more than a red ember. It would have finally gone out if the wind from the suddenly opened outer door had not forced it back into a

28

temporary white heat.

That same wind had an effect on the pool of kerosene which had been in the tin that Boroff's boot had kicked over. The liquid was impelled towards the tiny spot of incandescence.

Within three minutes, the entire floor was aflame. And hungry tongues were leaping round the base of the oil stove, where more kerosene was stored.

3

No Refuge

The pain in his ankle had faded. The tightness of his nerves had returned.

So Lieutenant Garnia was trying to obtain relief by writing a letter to his fiancée. He would not be able to post it for at least six weeks, not until he arrived back at base. But he found it comforting to begin a letter by writing an address at which he was not living and inscribing a date which had not yet arrived. Garnia found that the process gave an illusion that the worst was over and that he was finished with Post D.

My own darling Marie, he began.

But after that, words of ardour did not flow easily from his pen. The fact annoyed him, for Garnia was usually fluent in describing the unsullied joys which awaited the lady when she became his wife — an event which must wait until he attained the status and pay of a captain.

He sat haunched over his tiny desk, elbows on piles of official memoranda. He clicked his tongue and chewed his pen as he sought inspiration. After a while, he glanced at his wrist watch. Nine o'clock. And a storm outside. He listened to the storm.

It was weird. They were always weird, these Algerian desert storms. They made a man feel helpless. And this one had come more suddenly than most. Less than an hour's warning . . .

An idea occurred to him. It was staggering in its brilliant simplicity. It was the answer! It must be the storm which was making him feel so tense! *Mais oui!*

Garnia was a sensitive man. His inner senses were highly tuned. Without knowing it, he had sensed the approach of the storm long before it became apparent to cruder mortals! Garnia was elated by his own magnificent diagnosis. It made him want to laugh.

'*Dieu!*' he said. 'But I underestimate myself! I think I am a little psychic.'

The relief was enormous. Suddenly he

felt sleepy, all tension gone.

He undressed and put on the green silk pyjamas which Marie had given him. Then he threw himself onto his bunk.

★　★　★

There are sandstorms which kill. They rip the clothing off a man, tear his skin and block his breathing passages, so that he bleeds and chokes. And there are sandstorms, much the more frequent sort, which are little more than harsh inconveniences. This was one of that type.

Under its concealment, the three deserters had got over the low wall without difficulty and without being seen by the sentry who stood hunched on the rampart. Now, forearms shielding their eyes, they struggled south.

Katz shouted: 'This won't last. I know these storms. It will be gone in an hour. We will have covered twenty kilometres when dawn comes. Then we'll rest. We'll reach the oasis some time tomorrow.'

Hayle did not attempt to answer. He was scarcely aware of the German's presence, or of Boroff trudging slightly in the rear. He was hating himself.

A single stark accusation kept repeating in his mind. *You're a quitter . . . you're a quitter . . .*

Okay, so he'd quit. He couldn't take it. He guessed that other guys had quit before him. And for less reason. He wasn't running away from the Legion because he was soft, like Boroff. Or because the Legion had ceased to be useful to him, like that big German creep. No, sir! He had no real quarrel with the Legion. He had joined out of boredom and curiosity, and it hadn't been such a bad life.

But he had to get to the little town of Wichita, in Kansas. Had to cover those four thousand miles of land and ocean which divided him from his birthplace in the States. Had to . . .

★   ★   ★

A venerable alarm clock ticked competitively with the storm on the guardroom table. It was Corporal Jurgan's personal property and he was proud of it. He had bought it from a junk stall in the Arab market at Sidi bel Abbes years ago. It accompanied him everywhere. More than one inspecting officer had been startled to hear an apparently ominous ticking emerge from the corporal's pack before a route march. Jurgan obtained some additional satisfaction from the fact that he had placed the clock in the guard-room, for the use of all. It gave him the feeling of having done the Legion a favour.

He consulted the clock fondly before initialling the report sheet. It showed twenty-eight minutes to ten. But it gained fifteen minutes each day. And it was about twelve hours since it had been adjusted. Therefore Jurgan calculated that the correct time was nine twenty-five.

He beamed cheerfully about him. The stand-down guard of four men were dozing on the canvas wall bunks. They were nice fellows, he reflected. Rough and outspoken, perhaps. But full of solid virtue. It was so with all the rest of the garrison. Jurgan told himself that he was lucky to be senior N.C.O. in such a blissful post. It was stupid of Lieutenant Garnia to worry. There was nothing wrong with Post D . . .

The guard was not due to be changed until eleven o'clock. Jurgan had to supervise that. He decided to fill in the time in the mess room reading a new Dutch novel which he had received in a parcel before leaving base.

If he had not been shielding his eyes against the storm, he might have seen a glow which showed faintly through the kitchen window.

The mess room bunks were set in two rows against the walls. Jurgan's was in the centre of the row facing the door. From that position, he could keep a supervisory eye on all that occurred. After crossing to his bunk, Jurgan lit a small lamp on a shelf at the side of it — this was a privilege of his rank. Then he sat on a hard wooden chair (another privilege) and began reading his novel.

He had been doing this for a few minutes when he became aware of an irritation in his nostrils. He rubbed his plump nose vigorously. Then he glanced about him. Most of the men were sleeping, it seemed. But one or two were talking in a desultory fashion. Here and there a cigarette glowed in the gloom.

Then Jurgan realised that there was a taint of smoke in the air. At first he thought that perhaps one of the legionnaires was finding consolation in some exceptionally strong tobacco.

But a voice from one of the bunks asked: 'Who the hell's set fire to himself?'

It was only an idle, semi-joking enquiry. But it had Jurgan on his feet, sniffing vigorously. He moved to the big ceiling lamp, turning it full on.

He saw the billowing fumes emerging from under the kitchen door.

For a matter of seconds, Jurgan watched as if held by a hypnotic influence. Normally, Jurgan was an efficient N.C.O. Given an order, he could interpret it sensibly. He was familiar with every form of tactical manoeuvre which was likely to concern him. He knew his Manual of Regulations thoroughly. He could drill a squad on a parade ground with distinction.

But this was something entirely out of his experience. Once, long ago, he had taken a course in fire-fighting. But he had long since forgotten the lessons learned, for fire was not a normal hazard in the Algerian desert.

So Corporal Jurgan panicked. And he did the wrong thing. Without making any preparation for dealing with the flames, he rushed to the door and jerked it open. As he did so, he gave a moan, for the hot handle had scorched his hand. And a cloud of smoke and sparks drove into the mess room. Jurgan retreated before it.

Jurgan heard several legionnaires shout: 'Shut the door!' But now no one could get near it. Already the blankets on the bunks adjacent to it were alight, and the entire area had the temperature of a furnace.

★　★　★

For Lieutenant Garnia, it had been a delightful dream.

He had been with Marie in a heavenly

temple. Both of them were clothed in white raiments and they stood holding each other, listening to sweet and distant music. Then from somewhere came the drifting odour of incense . . .

Garnia woke spluttering because of the smoke in his throat. And immediately his eyes were moist and inflamed.

But it was to Garnia's credit that he did not lose his head. He was a volatile young man under normal circumstances, full of nerves and self-analysis. But he could be calm in an emergency.

He grabbed his slacks, tunic and kepi. He thrust his feet into his boots. Then, still clad in his green silk pyjamas, he picked up a chair and ran out into the compound.

There, dropping his uniform, he rushed to the kitchen window and threw the chair at it. Now, he told himself, it was possible to fight the flames without making the mistake of opening the doors.

He did not know that one door was already open. Or that part of the mess room was firmly alight.

The stand-down guard was running

towards him. One of the men held a fire bucket. Just one bucket. And that was a little more than half filled. A man might as well spit on the flames!

It was then that Garnia realised the preposterous inadequacy of the fire precautions at the post. One bucket of water in the guardroom! Two other buckets, he remembered, where in the kitchen itself, where they could not be reached. And the main drinking water tank was also in the kitchen . . .

They were helpless.

There could be no question of beating out the flames. All that could be done was to evacuate as much equipment as possible before the building was burned out.

The four men of the stand-down guard were grouped round him, blinking in stupefied bewilderment. He jerked a thumb at one of them.

He said: 'Tell Corporal Jurgan I want all the bunks and equipment moved out of the mess room.'

The man ran off. To the three others, Garnia said: 'We'll have to empty the magazine . . . if ten thousand rounds of ammunition and three hundred grenades go up . . . '

He did not finish the sentence. There was no need to. They knew what he meant.

Garnia led a race back to his room. From there they would somehow have to get the munitions out of the magazine. It would mean carrying them through a thick belt of smoke and heat. But it would have to be done.

But in the last two minutes, conditions had become much worse. When he had left it, the atmosphere in Garnia's room had been just barely breathable. It was no longer so.

The door dividing it from the kitchen was itself alight. Rivulets of burning oil were flowing along the floor.

Before they set a foot inside, they had to drop back. There was no possibility of forcing a way through. In there, the searing gases would burst a man's lungs, then shrivel him to a cinder.

Fascinated, Garnia watched the vital door which gave from his room into the magazine. He saw it through a vicious curtain of flame. For the moment it was intact. But that would not be for long . . .

And there was no other way into the magazine. For basic reasons, the post had been planned so that only the commanding officer had access to that vital place.

Garnia remembered that the roof of any building is usually its weakest point. Post D was no exception. It consisted of thin sandstone slabs laid over braced wooden beams. It might be possible to lever a few of the slabs out of place, thus making a hole big enough for a man to drop through. Then the munitions boxes could be lashed to ropes and hauled up.

It was a chance . . .

Garnia looked for the tallest of the three men. He recognised a bearded Pole, a gaunt and wiry man who stood inches over six feet.

'Get against the wall,' Garnia said. 'I'm going to stand on your shoulders.' The man understood immediately.

His green pyjamas waving grotesquely in the storm, Garnia kneeled first on the Pole's back, then stood on his shoulder blades. He balanced against the guttering. It was hot to the touch. With a thrust of his legs, he twisted on to the roof. This was hotter still. But he realised that the heat would be more intense here than in the kitchen, for there was an unbroken line of transmission. And the relatively thin slabs would warm more quickly than the thick walls.

Garnia tested one of the slabs with his fingers. Hopeless. There was not even room to place the tips beneath.

He bawled to the Pole: 'Your rifle — quick!'

The weapon was thrust to him. Crouching, he crashed the butt down. The sandstone did not so much as crack. He tried again. The same lack of result. The stuff was tougher — much tougher — than he had thought.

There was only one answer. It was a risk, but it had to be accepted. He decided to smash the slab by firing at it.

Garnia was uncomfortably aware that the hot slug *might* detonate the fused grenades if it entered one of the cases. But on the whole, the chances were against such a calamity, for the bullet would have to strike a single and infinitesimally small point on the ratchet pin. In any case, the grenades were stored along the wall. He must try to ensure that the shot did not fall near them.

The roof was built on only a very slight slope, so he was able to stand without difficulty. Then Garnia cocked the Lebel. He aimed vertically down. He squeezed the trigger.

Normally, the Lebel does not have a great recoil. Less than the Lee Enfield or the Mauser. Yet in this instance, it almost jumped out of Garnia's grasp. That was because the angle of fire had compelled him to lodge the butt partly under his armpit, from which position it easily jerked free.

But a jagged hole about three inches across had appeared in the centre of the slab. The rest of it was like shattered glass.

As he looked at the evidence of his minor success, Garnia waited for an explosion from below. None came. There was not time to be aware of any sensation of relief. He gestured to the Pole.

'You! Come up here! The others — get ropes from the guardroom!'

Garnia extended a hand and helped the bearded legionnaire onto the roof. As he did so, he wondered about Corporal Jurgan and the rest of the tiny garrison . . .

★   ★   ★

'The lieutenant says get the bunks and equipment out of here . . . '

Corporal Jurgan listened, palsied, to the order.

The lieutenant says . . .

In the name of God! How could he!

Already the flames had a grip on a good third of the room, and it was impossible to remain inside it. All of them were grouped just outside the door. They had retreated there just as the messenger had arrived.

Jurgan looked at the legionnaires. They made a sorry spectacle. All of them were grimed with smoke. Those whose bunks had been nearest the kitchen had been forced to withdraw so suddenly that they had lost even their rifles, their tunics, their boots.

Five of them were in that extreme condition. The remainder, including Jurgan himself, had been able to rescue their personal equipment, although some had been burned in the process.

Jurgan felt waves of humiliation and fury. They contrasted starkly with his normal good humour.

There was only one thing to do. He must report the facts to Garnia. Must tell him that a ghastly error had been made in opening that door. And that he himself had made it. Jurgan had his limitations, but he was a courageous and honest man.

But first he must take a roll call. It was no more than a formal precaution, for he knew that no one had been trapped in the room and that the kitchen was empty.

He gave an order. The legionnaires fell back across the open compound. They formed a single line under the west outer wall.

As he drew the roll from his breast pocket, Jurgan glanced back at the building. He saw the silhouette of Garnia and another man on the magazine roof. And he saw two other legionnaires running towards them with coils of rope.

The munitions! Of course, the munitions . . .

For a moment, Jurgan wondered whether to leave the roll call until later and deploy the men to assist Garnia. But he decided against it. That a man *might* be missing was no more than the vaguest possibility, but he could not afford to ignore it. Anyway, the work of calling a few names would not take more than half a minute.

It took slightly more than two minutes for Jurgan to establish beyond doubt that Legionnaires Hayle, Katz and Boroff were missing. Before arriving at the conclusion, he made a counter-check with the guardroom roster. There was no doubt of it. Eight men were on guard. That meant that twenty-three should be assembled in front of him. In fact, there were twenty.

He rapped a question: 'Have any of you seen these legionnaires?'

No one had. But a Bulgarian, one of those who was without rifle or adequate clothing, recalled seeing them talking together.

Jurgan sighed. This was beyond him. If the men were trapped, nothing could save them now. But he must tell Garnia. More evil news.

Scarcely noticing that the storm had almost passed, he ran towards the magazine.

★ ★ ★

Five stone slabs had been torn away. Garnia had dropped into the magazine.

He should not have done it. Smoke wafting up through the roof should have warned him. But he was driven by a frantic desperation.

Now he was standing in the centre of a furnace charged with cordite and lyddite. For even the door here was vanishing in flames. The square chamber glowed red. The redness gave a picturesque horror to the clouds of smoke. The heat dragged the juice from the lungs. Each intake of breath was an agony; a battle between a basic instinct and a natural fear.

He thought confusedly: *It's all over . . . all done. Post D is destroyed. I might as well stay here. If I do that, I'll be dead in a minute. No point in getting away. I'll be disgraced . . . there's no food . . . no water . . .*

No food, no water . . .

The significance of the two facts burst in his brain like the first stage of a fit.

They were hundreds of kilometres from base. And no means of keeping alive, save for the small amount of water each man always carried in his bottle and the tiny packs of emergency rations. There would be no shelter, either.

It was then that Garnia knew he must save himself, for his was the duty of saving the others.

A rope uncoiled from the hole above him. He reeled towards it.

On the roof, he coughed. Wild, uncontrollable paroxysms. He was only dimly aware that Corporal Jurgan was one of those who helped him to the ground.

Someone pushed a water bottle into his mouth. He flicked it away. Water was too precious.

Suddenly he could think again. Speak again. The agony in his chest had cleared.

Jurgan was saying: '*Mon officier* — I have to report that — '

'To hell with your report!' Garnia gasped. 'The magazine's going up! Get all the men outside the post. They must take cover behind the walls!'

★   ★   ★

There was nothing dramatic about the end of Post D. But it was very complete.

They knelt behind the south wall, near the gates. First they heard the thin popping of the cartridges. There would have been no need to retire if there had been only those to fear, for cartridges uncompressed by a rifle breech have little velocity. It was the grenades which mattered.

Those grenades — packed in ten cases of thirty each — seemed to explode simultaneously. They produced a boom akin to the distant firing of a *soixante-quinze* field gun. Most of the fragments slashed against the hot sides of the magazine. But others rose vertically. They pierced the roof or went freely through the hole in it. A few seconds later, they pattered down into the compound space. A few hot chunks dropped behind the garrison.

After that — nothing. Nothing save the crackle of fast-fading flames.

Without an order, as if by morbid instinct, they grouped together just inside the gates to watch the fire die out.

They stood thus and in silence for a long time, until nought but a few wisps of mocking smoke remained over a tragic skeleton.

It was then that Corporal Jurgan made his report.

4

The Meeting

A voice within her wild brain said: *Find them! Find them! They are killing your father . . .*

She tried to obey the prompting. She wanted to obey it. But she could see nothing save the swirling shroud of sand. Could hear nothing except the requiem of the wind.

In time — perhaps a matter of minutes, perhaps hours, it did not matter — she felt the strength flowing out of her body. She sank to the ground in a slight declivity. There she was shielded from the worst of the storm. And there she began to think clearly.

It was no use trying to find her father. He was dead. Killed like the others must have been.

At the realisation, she threw herself face down and wept into the dry and shifting sand.

When she raised her head again, the storm had all but gone. And in the light of a quarter-moon, she saw the tents of their camp a mere two hundred yards away. One of them had collapsed into a grotesque heap under the punishment of the wind. The others were inclining at stupid angles.

She must have been stumbling in circles.

Ruth moved towards the camp.

It was quiet. The Dylaks had gone. There was no sign of life. But there was evidence of death.

She almost stood upon her father's body before she saw it, for it had been covered by a layer of driven sand. She knelt and scraped the sand away. And when she saw what they had done to him, she shuddered and stood up. She raised a tiny fist to the sky. Her small breasts heaved. And there was fiendish fury in her begrimed face.

Then she went to the tents, composure returning.

The Dylaks seemed to have left most of the food. And there was water in plenty in the oasis well. But all the horses and mules had gone. That meant she would have to travel on foot to the Legion post which she knew lay almost due north. And she had heard that it was fifty-five kilometres distant. How far was that? Probably about thirty-five miles. A long way. But she would get there. She *had* to get there. And when the soldiers set out to find those Dylaks, she would go with them. Remain with them until the assassins were found.

But first there was other work to do.

In the equipment tent, she found a spade.

Dawn was breaking when she had covered over the temporary grave. Then she collapsed and slept.

★　★　★

Hayle said: 'It's way past midday and we've made good going.'

Katz snorted and wiped the bottom of his nostril with the back of his hand. It was one of his stock of obscene gestures.

'We're not resting yet,' he said. 'Not until I say we are to rest. So don't ask me. Save your strength.'

They plodded on for a few paces, tunics open to their bare chests, *kepis* pushed back from their filthy and unshaven faces.

Then Hayle said: 'I'm thinking about Boroff. He isn't lasting so well.'

Katz gave a contemptuous glance backwards. The Russian was indeed in a wretched state. He had dropped some twenty paces to the rear, and despite his occasional bursts of frantic speed, the distance between them was gradually increasing. His mouth was open. His eyes were glazed. His thin features looked as if they had been dipped in oil. Boroff, though a fit man by ordinary standards, lacked the normal toughness of his race. He could sustain an orthodox desert march with regular rest periods. But the pace that Katz was setting, plus the weight of an over-packed valise, was too much for him. He stared imploringly at the German.

Katz stopped. He said to Hayle: 'You

are right; Boroff has no stamina. Men without stamina are useless.' By his tones, he might have been discussing an unsatisfactory horse.

'He'll be okay if we lay up for a while,' Hayle suggested.

'Fool! We rest when we are at the oasis. Not before. I have decided that. There is no question about it.'

The German thrust forward his large slab-like face. Hayle regarded him coldly, dispassionately.

'Boroff won't be able to travel another couple of kilometres,' Hayle told him. 'So I guess you've no choice about it — we take a rest now.'

Katz tried to spit, but there was not enough moisture in his mouth to achieve this. He satisfied himself with the gesture and the sound effect. 'We can do without Boroff!'

'Do without him . . . Just what do you mean, Katz?'

'You know very well what I mean. Do you think I am stupid? I knew the pig would never survive!'

Hayle's voice became quiet. Ominously

quiet. He asked: 'Then why did you want to bring him with us, Katz?'

'That is a stupid question! The answer is plain. I wanted to bring him because he was the best man to get the food. He is small, he is quiet — like a miserable little mouse. And he has been able to carry equipment for us more than half of the way. That is a big help, is it not? It means more in reserve for us! I tell you, men such as us have to think of such things.'

When he finished, he was wearing a slight and utterly humourless smile. Hayle did not return it. Slowly, he groped in a pocket for one of his few cigarettes. He was lighting it when Boroff at last came up to them. He looked relieved to see that they had stopped.

'I'm . . . I'm glad we're resting,' he panted.

Hayle nodded. 'Yeah. We're resting, Boroff.'

The Russian threw his valise gratefully to the ground. His rifle followed. Then his ammunition pouches. He was unhooking his water bottle when Katz said: 'Our

American friend has made a mistake, Boroff. You may be resting, but *we* are not. We are going on.'

'I haven't made any mistake, Katz. All of us are squatting here for a while.'

Boroff was glancing frantically from one to the other. To him, the conflict was plain enough. But he did not yet recognise the vital part he was playing in it.

The caricature of a smile remained on Katz's wide, fleshy mouth. It tended to become more emphatic, showing the detail of his bad teeth. 'It makes no difference,' he said. 'We will do as I say. I, Hermann Katz, am the leader.'

The German flexed his right forearm. It was a massive forearm, almost as thick as an average man's thigh. Then he put a hand to the slide of his rifle sling. When the leather was slack, he slid the weapon over his head. He held it as if it was a puny toy.

Hayle had not moved. His cigarette was still between his lips. He asked gently: 'What are you going to do with that, Katz?'

There was a harsh clicking sound as Katz whipped back the Lebel bolt. Then he returned it to the breech, cocking the weapon. Holding the butt against his waist, he aimed it at Boroff.

He said: 'You cannot walk any further, can you, Boroff?'

At first the Russian did not answer. He stared in terror at the rifle muzzle. Then suddenly he shook his head, as if clearing it.

'Yes! Ah, yes, Katz! I'll be able to march well again after I've had a rest. Just a short rest . . . '

'*Ja!* I'm sure you could. But we cannot risk waiting here.'

'But . . . just an hour! It would not matter . . . '

'Perhaps not. But I will not take the risk, Boroff. I am going to get as far from the fort as I can before night comes.'

Pools of moisture formed in Boroff's eyes. His mouth was trembling. 'Is that why you're pointing your gun at me? Can it be . . . are you going to kill me? You can't do that, Katz! I've been a good friend to you!'

'But even good friends must part. Yet I am not going to kill you, Boroff . . . not unless you want me to kill you.'

Boroff pressed a trembling hand against his forehead. 'I don't understand! Of course I don't want to die!'

'Ah! You'll die in any case. But I am giving you a choice. *Nein!* I am giving you three choices, for I am a generous man. You can stay here alone and die of thirst. You can try to get back to the post. If you manage that, they will court-martial you and execute you. Or you can let me put a bullet through your forehead. Make up your mind, Boroff, for I cannot waste any more time! The choice is yours, my friend. But you will find a bullet from me the quicker and easier way.'

'But, Katz, I . . . '

'Feeble swine! Decide — or I will do it for you! You . . . '

Hayle interrupted. During the last minute, he had unslung his own Lebel. Quietly, he had cocked it. Now it was raised to shoulder. He was peering over the sights — at Katz.

And Hayle said: 'You might as well

relax, Katz! We're all going to take a rest
— just like I said.'

Katz half turned to face the American.
For a moment he seemed genuinely astonished at this challenge to his authority.
Then, under its dark tan, his face suffused
and his neck visibly swelled.

'Fool! Would you argue with me?'

'Yeah, I guess I would argue with you.'

'Put your gun down!'

'Sure. But you first, Katz.'

'Listen to me, my rash American
comrade — I am the leader here. It is I
who decides what is best. We want to get
away, do we not? We want to get to our
homes, don't we? Well, we are on our way.
The worst is over. Are you going to risk
seeing everything ruined because of this
miserable weakling?'

'He's still coming with us.'

Katz's Lebel was aimed from waist
level towards the pit of Hayle's stomach.
Hayle was aiming for the centre of the
German's contorted face. There was a
pause — brief but pregnant.

Katz broke it. He rasped: 'You
Americans are fond of what you call the

bluff. But you do not bluff me. I going to shoot Boroff — now!'

'Then you won't live long enough to see him die. Just as soon as you kill him, then I kill you.'

Katz's small round eyes became almost invisible. His forefinger tightened on the trigger. His gun was still directed at Hayle.

Hayle saw the fractional movement. He said: 'A bullet for a bullet, Katz. Squeeze that trigger just a little more, and I'll squeeze mine. I guess we'd both die at the same time.'

Katz did not answer. He remained very still.

Hayle's voice purred as he continued: 'Do you want to risk it, Katz? It'd be kind of funny if, after all, Boroff was the only one left alive.'

Katz lowered his rifle. He did so slowly, at first. Then, with a sudden savage gesture, he flung it to the ground.

They rested for nearly three hours, until Boroff was well able to continue. And during that time, none of them talked. The air was heavy with fear, fury and watchfulness.

It was Hayle who was watchful. He knew that from now on he would never be able to relax. Not while Katz was near him.

*   *   *

The sun was nearly down. Soon the swift twilight would be done and darkness would be on them.

They had made excellent progress. Boroff, spurred now by fear, had not lagged a step. They were within fifteen kilometres of the Lukka Oasis. But there was no point in trying to complete this last lap of the journey immediately. Even Katz was ready to rest during the night.

From the tops of their packs, they unstrapped their blankets. These were spread on the coarse red sand. They drank deeply from their water bottles — there was no need for caution with the oasis so near. Then they chewed goat meat and biscuits.

The tension between them had eased a little — but only a little. As they smoked after the meal, Hayle and Katz talked briefly, perfunctorily, about indifferent things. They ignored the crisis which was just over, though it was heavily on their minds.

Boroff was ridiculous, pathetic. His innate dread of Katz had increased tenfold. But it did not have the effect of driving him away from the German. The reverse.

In his terror, Boroff fawned upon Katz. Grovelled. Cringed. During the meal, he cut the German's meat into convenient morsels. He slackened the laces of his boots when Katz made a grumbling comment about the state of his feet. He gave one of his cigarettes to Katz. With trembling humility, he lighted it for him. If, at that time, Katz had kicked Boroff in the rear, the Russian would certainly have congratulated him on the accuracy of his aim.

It was completely dark save for the thin light from the crescent moon when Katz said: 'It is cold. We'll sleep better if we have a fire. There may be some dead camel thorn near. It makes a good fire.'

He trudged off.

Boroff gazed, fascinated, as the huge figure merged into the gloom. Then he whispered to Hayle: 'Listen! Is there really camel thorn about? Or is he going to shoot us?'

Hayle smiled. He made a gesture towards Katz's equipment. 'If he is, he'll have to manage without a gun. His rifle's there.'

Boroff gave a loud whimper of relief. Hayle added: 'What Katz says is right. There may be some dead cactus around because this is getting near the oasis. And it burns well.'

They sprawled on their blankets, waiting for Katz to return. They heard only the whisper of the breeze as it ceaselessly shifted the wastes of sand. And the distant squawk of a carrion bird on its way to roost among some rocks. That was all.

All, until Katz returned. He returned suddenly, half running.

Before they realised it, he was standing massively in front of them. Something lay across his arms. He dropped it to the ground. It rolled slightly and groaned. He gloated over it.

'Look, my friends!' he shouted. 'Look! This is what I have found . . . this is my own! A woman — a white woman!'

The pale moon was full on Katz's face. It showed a madness in his eyes.

5

Woman

She was conscious, but only barely so. Her linen shirt was torn. So were her breeches. Sand was in her fair hair. The strands splayed over her face.

Hayle kneeled beside her. He smoothed back the hair. She was looking at him, but in a hazy fashion. He felt awkward and afraid. He stood up and took a step toward Katz.

Hayle asked: 'How did you find her?'

Katz gave a titter. It sounded ludicrous in such a big man. 'She found me!'

'Quit stalling. What happened?'

'I heard something moving. I was surprised, but naturally. Yet I was careful. I kept still and I waited. She ran into my arms . . . *ha!* . . . my very eager arms!'

Hayle was bewildered. 'But where's she from? And how did she get here?'

'Be patient, my friend! That is something we will soon learn. She will tell us.'

'I'm thinking there must be others with her. She couldn't have come out to this area alone.'

'She is alone now. Look at her — she is lost. She is in despair. She is a woman . . . and I found her!'

She was drinking water from the bottle Boroff was holding to her lips. Her eyes were on Hayle. They had never left him. That haze had gone from them. She was recovering.

Her voice was surprisingly firm as she said: 'You're an American, I guess?'

He hoped he did not show the degree of astonishment that he felt. That once-familiar national accent came like a fluttering page of half-forgotten history. Or like a foretaste of the future. He tried to answer calmly.

'Sure am. I guess this is a strange kind of introduction, but I'm Hayle — Eddie Hayle.'

'I'm Ruth Westlake. You three are soldiers, aren't you? You're legionnaires.'

None of them answered. But she did

67

not seem to notice the constrained silence. She continued more easily: 'This is a break for me, finding you. I was trying to get to the Legion post, but I don't think I'd have made it. Are we far from the post?'

'You mean Post D?'

'Sure. It's the only one around these parts, isn't it? You'll be a patrol from it.'

Another pause, more tense than the last. Then Hayle said: 'Maybe you'd better tell us about yourself, Miss Westlake.'

He took a chance on using the unmarried title. She did not contradict him. But her face slackened, as if the muscles had become useless under the paralysing impact of a memory.

She said softly: 'Of course, you'll want to know. It must seem kind of weird finding me all alone in this part of Algeria.' She looked at Hayle's cigarette. Then she added: 'A smoke would help.'

He gave her one. The tobacco was dark and strong. She coughed at first. Hayle said: 'They got me like that the first time I used them. But they're about the only sort we can get. You get used to them.'

She smiled faintly. By now she was sitting upright, her slim back half supported by a valise.

Katz had been following the conversation with difficulty and mounting annoyance. He strode forward until he stood directly over her. He rasped: 'Don't forget me, *fräulein!* I am Katz. I am Hermann Katz. I found you. When you talk, you will talk to me, too.'

She looked up at him, puzzled. 'Are you in charge of this patrol?'

'I am in charge.'

Hayle cut in. He said: 'Just tell us your story, Miss Westlake. Tell it to *all* of us.'

She talked. When she described the death of her father and the other archaeologists, she was near to tears. But when she mentioned the Dylaks, there was an aura of ferocity about her. As she finished her story, she stood up, defying her exhaustion. She showed an almost feline intensity.

'Now you know why you must take me to the Legion post at once,' she said. 'Time is so precious! Those killers are getting further away with every hour that passes!' She looked hard at each of them. Then she tossed down her cigarette.

The three men stood hunched before her. None of them moved. The only sound was a nervous sniff from Boroff.

Suddenly, she appeared to realise that something was wrong. 'What's the matter?'

None of them attempted an answer.

'Why do you look at me like that?'

Still silence.

'You . . . you *are* legionnaires, aren't you?'

Hayle felt compelled to end her agonised uncertainty. The brutal truth could be no worse for her than this. 'Yes,' he said. 'We are legionnaires.'

Momentarily, she showed relief. 'Then you'll understand that your patrol — '

'We're not a patrol.'

'Say . . . say that again?'

'We're not a patrol.'

'But I don't understand. If you're not on duty, what are you doing out here?'

Before Hayle could answer, Katz gave an astringent laugh. He spoke as though thoroughly enjoying the process.

'Listen, *fräulein*. You will find this interesting, I think. You see three legionnaires here. Anyway, you see three men in Legion uniform. But we are deserters. Yes, deserters from Post D. We cannot go back. *Nein!* Not even for a bereaved American woman!'

Slowly, she turned towards Hayle. She looked full at him. He had to lower his eyes.

'It's true,' he said, while gazing at the ground. 'We can't go back.'

She put her two hands together. She did so to stop them trembling. Then she said to Hayle: 'I ought to be able to talk to you straight — both being Americans.'

'I guess so.'

'Then you must realise that I've got to reach the post. And I know now I can't do it alone. Walking over this territory's a lot rougher than I thought. Won't you escort me at least part of the way, so I get the worst over?'

A throaty, bellowing laugh smote the night air. It came from Katz. 'You have nerve, *fräulein*! You expect us to walk into the arms of a search party just to oblige you! Do you know what will happen to us if we are captured? I will tell you. We will be executed! Put up against a wall and shot!'

She glanced at Katz with almost open disgust. He caught the expression and his good humour vanished. Then she squared her shoulders.

'Okay — I'll have to go on alone and hope for the best. I guess I might be lucky and run into the search party that's looking for you.'

'That,' Katz said deliberately, 'is one reason why we cannot let you go, *fräulein*.'

'You can't let me go?'

'*Ja*, that is right.'

'Look — we're going to get one thing straight, and we're going to do it right now. Understand this — I'm a United States citizen and I'm in French territory under a legitimate American passport. If the thugs who killed my father aren't brought to justice, there'll be trouble enough from Washington. But if you start trying to interfere with my liberty, there'll be an international incident. While I'm here, I'm entitled to French protection, and I'm not going to be molested!'

She was breathless when she finished. The humourless smile was back on Katz's slab-like face.

'That was a nice speech, *fräulein*. But does it frighten me? *Nein!* If you were the president of the United States, I would not let you go! Don't you see what would happen if you did make contact with the post? A patrol would be sent out to the oasis to investigate. They would stay there for days. A wireless signal would be sent to base. Then, perhaps, aeroplanes would fly out to Lukka Oasis, bringing more investigators. We'd be finished! Done!'

'But I wouldn't tell them about you. It's no business of mine that you're deserters. I'd— '

'Fool! They would not spread all over the oasis because of us. It would be because your precious American citizens had been killed. But we would not be able to camp there and wait for an Arab caravan, as we had planned. We would have to give ourselves up, or die of thirst.

Now do you understand, *fräulein*?'

She put a hand to her slender throat. After what seemed a long time, she nodded. 'I understand. Because . . . because I've run into a bunch of quitters, the mob who killed four harmless men are to be allowed to escape!'

'That is so, *fräulein*.'

'Then, if you won't let me go on — what are you going to do with me?'

Katz laughed again. 'What am I going to do with you? You are my own responsibility, *fräulein*. It was I who found you. Don't forget that.'

★ ★ ★

Lieutenant Garnia retired to a discreet corner of the compound. There he took off his green silk pyjamas and put on his uniform — or those parts of his uniform which he had salvaged during his retreat from his room. Outwardly he was reasonably complete, except that his belt, pistol and holster were missing. But lacking a shirt, his tunic was in direct contact with his skin. It chafed

74

uncomfortably. He had no socks, either. But that was a deficiency he could probably remedy by a loan from one of the legionnaires. They usually had two or three spare pairs.

An acrid smell drifted from the burnt-out building. He sniffed it wearily, like a man performing an unpleasant duty. He saw the silhouettes of the legionnaires who were searching the place. They were not likely to find anything. Garnia thought that he would be the most surprised man in all Algeria if they discovered the remains of the three missing legionnaires. As soon as Jurgan had made his report on them, Garnia had realised that it was most unlikely they had been trapped by the flames. It was just possible that *one* man might be trapped and his cries unheard. But that it should happen to *three* of them was unthinkable. It was obvious to him that they had deserted. And he would not be surprised if the fire and the desertions were not in some way connected.

But for the time being, the deserters were the least of his worries. Garnia produced a notebook and pencil from his breast pocket. Leaning against the wall, he began to scribble. He was enumerating the problems confronting him. He found that the mere act of setting down difficulties in writing tended to clarify them.

First — he had twenty-nine men under his command, allowing for the three absentees. Twenty-seven of them were armed and had their full personal allotment of one hundred and twenty rounds of ammunition. These men also had full water-bottles (about three pints) and iron rations to last two days. The five others had lost almost everything in the fire — their rifles, water, food. Even their boots. They were a liability on an already desperately situated squad of men.

There had been no time to radio a message to base. Therefore, their plight was unsuspected by those who could send help. A routine check signal was made every ten days. The next one was not due for a week. It would be a week, therefore, before base began to question what was happening at Post D. And even then it was unlikely that they would take immediate action, for they would imagine that the post's radio transmitter had developed a defect. In the unlikely event of their sending any extra routine signals and receiving no reply, they would come to the same conclusion. Therefore, it would most likely be more than a week before base became really worried.

Garnia bit his lip as he scrawled down the unhappy facts. They had food and water for about two days. They must arrange to survive for at least two weeks. That was the quintessence of the problem. There was no possibility of staying within the ruined post. Where to go?

Garnia closed his eyes. He wished he had his charts. He had to rely on his memory.

It was no effort to recall the Lukka Oasis. It was the nearest and most obvious place. There they would have water. And there was a good chance of a caravan passing and providing them with food.

Garnia suddenly ceased to write. A

forgotten fact came flooding back into his mind. Before setting out to take over the post, he had been given the usual Memorandum of Instructions. The type-written sheets had contained a paragraph headed *Archaeological Expedition*. This had aroused his passing interest because it was unusual. The paragraph had stated that an American expedition was assembling supplies and bearers at Reggan before proceeding to . . . Lukka!

He could not recall the exact dates involved. But he was sure that the expedition would be at the oasis at this very moment. In fact, it had been at the back of his mind that he must send out a patrol to make a routine check on the place.

Dieu! They were saved!

The expedition would have food, clothing, everything. Perhaps even a radio transmitter, though on the whole he doubted that. He had gathered that it was a small expedition. As such, they would be unlikely to carry the bulky radio equipment needed for long-distance transmissions.

But that did not matter much. The important fact was that suddenly a very serious problem had dissolved into nothing. Or nearly nothing.

He would leave a written message at post — something big, which could also be read from the air in case a reconnaissance plane was sent over first; then wait at the oasis for help to arrive.

It crossed his mind that when they had rested and taken in supplies from the archaeologists, he might march back to base immediately. But he dismissed this notion. He was still responsible for law and order in the area. Therefore, he must remain within it until given proper relief.

Bon! As soon as dawn broke, they would start for Lukka.

Garnia was still congratulating himself when Corporal Jurgan appeared. The worried and chagrined Jurgan was almost unrecognisable from his normal beaming self.

He said: 'You were right, *mon officier*. The three men were not trapped in the flames, for there is no sign of them. They must have deserted.'

Garnia ignored the information. He was not interested in it. He embarked immediately on an explanation of his plan, emphasising the points with vivid gesticulations. Garnia was one of those Latins who would be struck dumb if his hands were tied together.

Jurgan, who had been unaware of the existence of the archaeological expedition, listened with astonished relief. 'Then we will survive, *mon officier!*'

'We have nothing to worry about. We will survive.'

'And as soon as it's light, we fall back south to join the people at Lukka.'

'Did you say *fall back?* I do not like that phrase, corporal! It is not proper to our traditions. We are not running away from anything. *Non.* We are simply taking up new positions. At dawn we *advance* south!'

* * *

Sixty kilometres west of the Lukka Oasis, the trading caravan of Ata Masit was plodding its way heavily towards the far distant borders of French Sudan. They hoped to sight the northern loop of the River Niger in about a month.

Then they would work down the banks of the river, trading in the villages. Their blades and silks would bartered for ivory, food and a little gold. Eventually they would strike the great caravan centre of Timbuktu, where they would rest awhile before again setting forth acre the Sahara to their homes under the brooding shadow of the Atlas Mountains. The round journey took nearly six months to complete. Masit and his forty men did it once each year.

They were about to pitch camp for the night when they saw the Dylaks, who were doing the same. But it was not the Dylaks alone which attracted the interest of the shrewd Ata Masit. He was also interested in the five magnificent horses which they had with them. And the twelve lightly laden pack mules.

The Dylak people, Masit knew well enough, did not usually possess such material riches. They were warlike by instinct, and when they toiled, it was reluctantly and in a humble capacity. What, then, were they doing with the animals?

Masit's string of trading camels bore down on the Dylaks. It was a cautious meeting. The ferocious Dylaks formed themselves into a circle, fingering their knives. Masit raised a hand in a gesture of peace. Although he outnumbered them by two to one, he certainly did not want a quarrel with such warriors as these.

Slowly — for he was no longer a young man — Masit descended from his kneeling camel. 'Ala Masit, the great trader, greets you,' he announced. 'We are bound for the Niger and we travel in peace.'

The Dylaks relaxed slightly. But they remained watchful.

Masit continued: 'You have mules which I am ready to buy, for my own beasts are already overburdened.'

It was a piece of cunning on Masit's part to state his interest so quickly. He knew that the un-business-like Dylaks would be moved to immediate interest at the prospect of converting their surplus mules into money, even though they would probably get a far higher price if they waited.

After a short hesitation, one of the Dylaks said: 'We welcome you, Masit . . . '

Two hours later, Masit had extracted the whole story of the massacre at Lukka from the Dylaks. He did so bit by bit, as they ate together and drank thick, sweet coffee. It was not a difficult process, for the Dylaks could scarcely forbear to boast of what they considered a superb achievement.

The facts caused Masit to ponder very hard. For the slaughtered Americans he had no sympathy. Neither did he bear them any acrimony. It was their misfortune to have found gold at the oasis while relying on the integrity of members of a tribe to whom the word had no meaning. They had paid logically for their rashness.

But it occurred to Masit that where coins had already been found, more of them might still remain. It would be worth a little digging to see.

And the Dylaks had been quite open

about the fact that they had left many of the white men's stores at the oasis, taking with them only what they needed when they fled. That was typical of the Dylaks. But it also meant tin there would be many rich pickings if he got there quickly.

'I will buy six of your mules,' Masit said.

After some unskilled haggling on the part of the Dylaks, the price was fixed.

They parted when dawn came.

As soon as the Dylaks were out of sight, Masit changed the course of his caravan and made swiftly towards the Lukka Oasis.

He was resolved that even if he found others there before him, he would fight them if need be, for his men were we armed and they were brave. Nothing was going to prevent him acquiring what remained of the white men's stores. And perhaps finding gold, too.

6

Desired

Katz said: 'You are back, my fair *fräulein*. But it does not look good to you, uh? I am sorry. Very sorry. My warm heart . . . '

'Shut up!'

'So Legionnaire Hayle is annoyed, eh? Then I will leave him. I will inspect the stores. But do not talk too intimately with your fellow American. Remember — it was I who found her. It is I who will look after her.'

Katz stamped out of the tent. Ruth, slumped in a canvas chair, watched him go. Hate and fear were in her eyes.

She said to Hayle: 'I suppose in one way I ought to be grateful to you.'

He was leaning against the tent's centre pole. There was an air of weary confusion about him.

'Grateful to me? Why?'

'If you weren't here, I'd be due for a lot

of trouble with that big gorilla.'

'Maybe. I guess I can hold him off.'

She looked through the tent flap. She saw the ugly mounds which marked the excavation site. Subconsciously, her eyes followed the path which her father had taken on that last ghastly rush of his. She stared at the place where her aching arms had made a temporary grave.

Ruth shuddered. In the last two days, horror had mingled with horror so that she felt herself clothed in a haze of unreality. As if her tortured mind would soon reach a point where it would cease to react. Where nothing would mean anything.

She asked: 'Now that you've brought me back here, maybe you'll tell me what's going to happen.'

He did not look at her. 'You'll be okay. No one'll touch you. I'll see to that.'

'I'm not thinking about that. I'm thinking about what's going to become of me when you clear out of here — when a caravan comes and takes you into Spanish territory.'

'We'll take you with us, I guess. We

can't leave you here.'

'And then?'

'We're aiming to reach the Spanish Sahara port of Vil Cisneros. There we find a ship and work our way home.'

'Do you expect me to do the same?'

'No. I figure there'll be an American consulate in the town. They'll see you okay.'

'Doesn't that make you afraid for yourselves?'

'Why should it?'

'When I explain to the United States consul what happened to me, he'll most likely ask the Spanish authorities to put you all under arrest. Then you'll be handed back to the Legion.'

Hayle glanced at her thoughtfully. He gave a strained smile.

'The Spanish wouldn't hand us back. Legion deserters have gotten over that border before. They're interned for a while, then deported home. But we don't plan to fall into their hands. We'll have to ask for your word that you'll say nothing about us until we're well clear of the place.'

Suddenly she was watching him carefully. With interest. 'You trust me that far?'

'Why not? You're an American. So am I. This uniform can't alter that.'

'Will Katz trust me?'

'To hell with Katz!'

She dabbed her face with a soiled handkerchief. Then she said precisely: 'It's not as easy as that, is it? Anyone can see what Katz is. He's a brute. He's very dangerous. You don't want me to think so, but you're afraid of what he might try to do.'

Hayle felt himself compelled to meet the challenge of her eyes. They were strong blue eyes, set in a face which had intelligence as well as beauty. This woman shouldn't be out here, suffering, and at the mercy of three Legion quitters! She should be back home in the States. Just out of college, maybe, and going to parties with moonlight drives afterwards. Making the guys turn their heads when she swept down the sidewalks. That was where she ought to be. But it was all wrong. Why did she have to be here and make things even worse than they were?

She was repeating her statement. '. . . you're afraid of what he might try to do . . .'

He said almost savagely: 'I'm not scared of Katz!'

'I didn't say that, and I don't think you are. There's a big difference between fearing what a brute may do and being afraid of the brute himself.'

Hayle shook his head. He spoke roughly. 'You're playing around with words. I'm not interested. I've told you you'll be okay. Now relax.'

They were silent for several minutes. From some way off, they could hear Katz swearing at Boroff. They were examining the stores.

Then she said: 'Mind if I ask you something — something kind of personal?'

'No. I don't need to answer. I don't even need to give you the truth.'

'You won't feed me any lies. I know your type. How come you're quitting the Legion? And what made you enlist, anyway?'

He fumbled for a cigarette, then decided against taking one. He had only three left. Those eyes of hers never left him. They made him feel uncomfortable, yet at the same time a little flattered.

'Y'know something,' he said, trying to speak easily, 'every European tourist who's ever met up with a legionnaire asks him why he enlisted. It happens in Marseilles, it happens in Algiers, it happens in Bel Abbes. They buy the guy a drink, then think they've got a copyright on his life history. 'Tell me, my man,' they say, 'what goddamned awful tragedy put you into the Legion?' It makes us all sick!'

Her expression did not alter. 'I'm no tourist,' she said. 'And I'm not sitting in an Algiers cafe, either. But since I'm relying on you for my life, you're rather important to me. So it's only natural I want to know something about you.'

He jerked himself away from the tent pole and walked to the flap. Katz and Boroff were a hundred yards away. Boroff was dragging packing cases from under a canvas cover. Katz was listing them and their contents. He was thorough man, was Katz.

With his back to her, he said: 'Okay. You can have my story, Miss Westlake. It won't take long to tell.'

'The name's Ruth. It'd make things easier if you used it — Eddie.'

He pretended not to hear. He turned abruptly to her, his tall frame tense. His voice was harsh again as he asked: 'Are you proud of the United States Air Force?'

She nodded slowly.

'I'm glad,' Hayle told her, 'because I guess that gives us something else in common. I was a captain in that outfit — until four years ago.'

'Why did you leave it? Did you — '

'No, I didn't get drunk and sock a general. I didn't even run into debt and steal Army dough. I left it to run a drug store in Wichita!'

There was the merest trace of a smile on her face. 'A drug store!'

'Sure. It was a family business. My pop — he died. There was no one else to take it over, so I had to step in.'

'And you didn't like it?'

'I hated it. Drove me crazy. And you know what? When I was in charge, the place started to lose money!'

'I guess it would, if you hated it.'

'But I had to hold on because it was the only support for my mother. Then one day I saw the way out. A big conglomerate offered to buy the store. The price was good. And they were ready to make a regular extra payment to my mother. I put the deal through and turned over all the dough to the old lady; that saw her okay. Then I tried to get back in the service. They wouldn't take me. Y'know why? Because I'd already had a compassionate discharge for family reasons. They figured I wasn't a very reliable proposition. Standards are high in the Air Force.'

'So you came to Europe and enlisted in the Foreign Legion?'

'That's about it. I was feeling sore. I was looking for some action. The Indo-China war was on then. I figured I might be sent there. But instead I spent all my time in Morocco and Algeria. I'm not beefing, though. The Legion's like most other armies, except that it's an international force. If a guy plays square in the Legion, then the Legion plays square with him.'

She leaned forward to him, a hand on her small chin. 'And what put you wrong?'

It wasn't the Legion.'

'I thought it couldn't be.'

He paused and swallowed at a lump in his throat. His face had coloured. 'It's my mother. She's sick. Very sick. I got a cable when we were back at base. It nearly drove me nuts. I got an interview with the colonel. I told him I'd come back; I pledged my word. I just wanted to get home, just for a while. You see, she's asking for me. But it was no good. Oh, I don't blame the colonel. He was a good guy. It was just that he had no power to release me. No one had. Once you're in the Legion, you've got to stick in it until your five years are up. Now . . . now I guess you know it all.'

She was on her feet, moving towards him. She put a hand on his. It felt light and smooth. 'I'm sorry,' she said.

'Sorry for what?'

'Sorry that I called you a quitter. You're not quitting from anything, Eddie.'

Suddenly he felt weak. He had an urgent desire to hold her; to press her against him and bawl like a kid. Not because she was young and lovely and good to hold. But because she was a woman. And there are some things a woman understands better than any man.

He jerked away from her, and strode out of the tent and towards Katz and Boroff.

This woman had troubles enough of her own . . .

★   ★   ★

At mid-afternoon, Hayle, Boroff and Katz held a conference in what had been Dr. Westlake's tent. Katz, as usual, did most of the talking.

'We come here to find many cases of food,' he said. 'Enough to feed us for months. You think we are lucky. *Ja*, we are lucky. But only in one way, my friends. We are waiting for an Arab trading caravan to pass this way so as to take us into Spanish Sahara. What happens when such a caravan does come?' He glared round at them, big jowls expanded.

'You tell us,' Hayle said. 'What happens?'

Katz crashed a fist on to the small table. The flimsy piece of furniture almost collapsed under the blow.

'The Arabs will take the stores! They will be delighted! But will they take us? *Nein!* There will be no room for us on their camels and mules. We will be left here, my friends!'

They considered the point. It was of obvious validity.

Katz continued: 'I have been thinking.' He tapped his forehead significantly 'It is fortunate for you that my brain is quick. First, I wondered if it was possible to reach Spanish territory on foot. But plainly it is not. The distance is too great. We would perish. We must have animal transport. Then I saw the answer. It is this — when the first Arabs come this way, we will not plead with them! We will shoot those on the best camels. The others will run off. Then we will have mounts of our own. We will get to Spanish territory quickly and safely. That is clever, is it not?'

Boroff nodded eagerly. 'It is very clever, Katz. It is a bold plan. Just the sort of plan we would expect from you.'

Hayle was tilted back in his chair, hands thrust into the pockets of his slacks. He did not speak.

'Well, my American friend! Do you not agree with your friend Boroff that I have thought of a master plan?'

Still Hayle remained silent. But his eyes were fixed firmly on the German.

'Answer me! Don't stare at me like a fool!'

Hayle shrugged his shoulders slightly. He said in a casual way: 'You're a killer, aren't you, Katz? You're the complete, stinking article.'

Katz kicked back the chair. He circled the table, bunching his fists. Hayle remained in the chair.

'No one talks to me in such a way! You push me too far, my friend! I will have to show you how foolish you have been!'

'*Sit down!*' Hayle shouted the two words. It was a full-blooded shout. It matched in volume Katz's own bellowing efforts.

Katz looked astonished. 'What — what was it you said to me?'

'You heard, you muscle-bound oaf!'

'Muscle . . . '

'Yeah, muscle-bound. Now get this straight. If you want to go in for strong-man games, I'm ready to play. But we're not going to get anywhere that way. So get back in your chair and listen to me for a change!'

Katz's appearance was reminiscent of a simmering kettle. The lid threatened to blow off. But it got no further than a threat. He said: 'Very well. It would be stupid of us to fight now. I will hear what you have to say.'

He went back to his chair. And Hayle knew he had won an important battle. He had staked everything on his knowledge of this particular type of Teutonic character and had not been mistaken. Katz had an immediate respect for anyone who could shout louder than he.

Hayle said, when they were composed again: 'We're not going to murder Arabs. We haven't killed anyone yet, and we aren't going to start if we can help it.'

'But it is the only way. The Arabs will — '

'I know. You've said it before, Katz. The Arabs will take the stores and leave us here. But I figure it a different way.'

'So! And what is it that you figure?'

'That it's best to fix things so that the Arabs can't see the stores. We'll bury them. Anyway, bury most of them, just keeping around us what we need. Maybe we keep one or two things as gifts for the Arabs. But there won't be so much loot for them that they can't carry us along. D'you understand, Katz?'

'*Ja*, I understand. But as a plan it is weak! Weak, I tell you! We are well armed, are we not? It is more sensible — more logical — for us to use our Lebels to get camels of our own. Why? Because a caravan moves slowly. *Ja!* Very slowly. But we on our own could travel fast.'

Boroff was sitting between them. His

thin voice piped: 'You are right, Katz! Speed is what we need.'

But his grovelling contribution was ignored by both men. Boroff had the dubious distinction of being unwanted as an ally and unfeared as an enemy.

'There'll be no shooting,' Hayle said. 'Maybe you'll find it an inconvenience, Katz, but that can't be helped. We'll do it my way and we'll start right now.'

Katz drummed his fingers on the table. Then he said: 'You are squeamish, my friend. You are weak, like many Americans. But we must stand together. So I will give way to you. We will hide the stores. But there are a lot of them. It will take days, perhaps.'

'It won't take us more than a couple of hours.'

'So! And what — what miracle have you in mind?'

'No miracle. We'll just dump them in the ditch left by the excavators and cover it over. That won't take long.'

Katz stood up abruptly. He peeled off his tunic and slapped his massive and hair-matted torso. 'Then let us get spades and start,' he said.

The work took rather longer than Hayle had estimated. There were unexpected delays. These arose over the question of what should be retained for their own use. Hayle was in favour of keeping this down to a minimum. Katz, and, of course Baroff, were not. They compromised, retaining two cases of tinned food, a sack of coffee, plus a highly expensive Sperry gyrostatic compass. The compass was intended as a gift for the Arabs. It was doubtful whether they would know how to use it. And certainly they would not need it. But it was the type of complex article which would fascinate and impress them.

As they dumped the rest of the supplies, Hayle saw his first visible evidence of the massacre. There were blood splashes on the ancient stone remains. For a moment, he wondered where the bodies were. Then he saw a patch of recently disturbed sand nearby. There had been a pathetic attempt to put a headstone, in the form of a slab of rock, over it. He remembered what Ruth had told him. She had done that alone. Four men! He felt a fresh surge of respect for her.

They were breathing hard and soaked in sweat when at last the job was done. They had not attempted to fill in all the excavations; that would have taken days. Only that part where they had dumped the cases with unwanted tents and articles of furniture. But even so, it had been exhausting in the torrid atmosphere.

As they returned to their tent, Hayle said: 'We'll have to tell the first caravan that comes that we found the relics of a digging expedition.'

Katz asked: 'What of the woman? Will she tell them the truth? I have just thought she might let them know what we have done!'

'She won't.'

'What makes you so sure, my friend?'

'Plenty of reasons that you wouldn't understand. But I guess you appreciate this one — she wants to get out of here herself.'

'You think we are taking her with us, uh?'

Involuntarily, the two men stopped. They faced each other.

Hayle said slowly: 'Had you anything else in mind, Katz?'

Katz rubbed his black-bristled chin. '*Nein.*'

'I'm glad. Now, let's get some rest. We need it.'

★   ★   ★

Hayle had intended only to doze on the camp bed — and to keep an eye on Katz, who was sprawled near the open flap. That had been his intention. But exhaustion and worry pulled him away from the realm of consciousness.

Katz had been watching him. Watching Boroff, too, who also slept. And when he judged it safe, Katz rose. He pushed out of the tent and strode deliberately towards Ruth's.

She heard the steps approaching over the rocky sand. At first she thought it was Hayle, and she was glad.

A moment later she knew the first flicker of fear. They were very heavy steps.

Heavier than the American's.

She had been sitting on the edge of her bed, thinking about her father, about the Dylaks, about Hayle; all in a muddled, disconnected way. Now suddenly her mind was clear, alert. She stood up, knowing who to expect before the ponderous figure became visible.

Katz seemed to crash through the tent flap rather than walk through it. Just inside he stopped, blinking in the relative gloom. 'Don't be afraid, *fräulein*,' he said. 'I will not hurt you.'

The back of her throat had become very dry. But she said steadily: 'Will you please get out of here. If you want to talk to me, you can do so later, when the others are around.'

He grimaced. It was no more than a grimace, but somehow he inserted something vaguely indecent into it. 'But you did not mind speaking alone with the American!'

'That's because he's an American, and so am I.'

Katz moved ponderously into the tent, but he did not attempt to get close to her.

He stopped beside a box which contained some of her personal possessions. He sat on it.

Her eyes were open wide as she watched him and became aware of his basic animalism. It showed in his huge muscles. His utterly straight mouth. The acrid smell of sweat from his bare torso. The fact that he had a brain — probably a good brain — made his menace the more complete.

Katz was aware of the impact he was causing. He took his time before speaking. Then he said: 'You are making a mistake, *fräulein*, if you rely on your fellow American. It is I who must look after you.'

'I can look after myself.'

He gave a brief laugh. 'Now you are foolish and proud. But never mind. I — how is it you say? — *Ja!* I go for proud women.'

She thrust her hands into the pockets of her jodhpurs. 'Maybe. But I don't go for you. Now get out of here, or I'll — '

'Or you'll shout for your friend? Your American friend! Is that what you were going to say, *freulein*?'

He was regarding her with possessed insolence. The sense of fear within her increased. She could only nod.

'Please don't do that, *fräulein*. Not until you have heard what I have to say. Then I don't think you will want to call for him.'

'Okay. What is it you have to say?'

'You know we may be waiting at this oasis for many days — perhaps even weeks? Caravans pass this way — *ja!* But we may have to wait for the right one. The one that takes us into Spanish Sahara.'

'I know that. You're not telling me anything new.'

'But you are going to be in a difficult position, *fräulein*! Had you thought of that? I think you must have done so, for you are not a child! One very beautiful woman . . . just one . . . sharing a camp with three very rough men . . . ' He finished with an expressive wave of a huge hand.

She knew what he was going to say. But she felt compelled to hear him say it. 'Go on. I'm listening.'

'*Fräulein* . . . even three saints would quarrel over you if they were forced to live in such a way. We are not saints. We are men! And I, Hermann Katz, am the best man of all! So I think it would save a lot of trouble if you decided in favour of one of us. The others would be disappointed, of course. But they would have to endure that. I am thinking, *fräulein*, you would be wise to choose me! I am — '

'Get out, you scum — out of here before scream!'

Her entire slender body was trembling. Her face drained white.

'Wait! You have not heard everything. You want the American to live, don't you?'

She framed the word deliberately before repeating it. 'Live . . . of course I want him to live.'

'Good! It is as I thought. He will live if you do as I say. But if you try to seek his protection, then I will kill him. *Ja* — I will do that.'

She sobbed for a moment. Then she whispered: 'You wouldn't dare to try that.

He might kill you.'

'He might kill me — in a fair fight. But I would not take that risk. I would wait until he slept, as he is sleeping now. Then . . . my bayonet in his throat, perhaps. Or a shot in his head!'

'You — you're very sure of yourself. How do you know he won't do that first?'

'How? That is so simple. Legionnaire Hayle is a squeamish man — I have just told him so. He will not kill. He will not even kill Arabs! But I do not have such a handicap, *fräulein*. It is good to be strong. It has many advantages.'

As he finished, Katz stood up. He slapped his glistening chest with an open palm. It produced a sound like a pistol shot.

She wanted to back away, but was already close to the tent wall. She wanted to cry out, but instinct told her that it would be the wrong thing to do. She needed time — time to think. Just a few minutes during which she could seek a way of handling this repulsive man.

It was intuition — pure feminine intuition — which prompted her to appeal to his vanity. She said softly, as if succumbing to a reluctant interest: 'You must have had a very unusual life to face up to things the ways you do.'

'*Ja*. It is so.'

'You're a bitter man. Like one who's suffered a lot.'

He smiled. With lewd deliberation, he spat on the floor. 'I have not suffered much, *fräulein*. Others can suffer — but not I!'

'I can't believe that! Everyone — even a man like you — has a weak spot somewhere.'

'*Nein!* I know of no weakness in me. If you had seen what I have seen and done what I have done, you would understand!' He finished with a significant smile. She took the cue.

'What have you done? What is it that makes you so different from other men?'

Katz hesitated. He regarded her with a form of primary concentration, like a cautious bull analysing a matador. Then he said: 'Perhaps you would like me still less if I told you.'

'Perhaps. But I guess you're the type of

man to that risk.'

'*Ja*. I think I am. So I will tell you. Now look at me, my *fräulein*! Look into my eyes!'

He compelled her obedience. There was cold coercion in his jarring tones. She had to mobilise all her willpower to avoid giving a gasp of terror as she met his eyes. It was the first time she had seen them properly. They did not mirror life. They were the eyes of one who is dead. Flat, unblinking, without a connecting soul.

'My eyes frighten you, *fräulein*. You need not be ashamed. They have frightened others stronger than you.' He broke off and drew himself to his full height. He stretched his hands down the sides of his trousers, assuming the position of attention.

Then he added: 'I have another name — a real name, and it is not Hermann Katz. But that does not matter. I — I was once *untergruppenfuehrer* in Heinrich Himmler's S.S. Once I served the Reich in the camps of Dachau and Buchenwald. Once I was a personal bodyguard to Himmler himself!'

Ruth thought: *This should be the final shock. This should make me feel ill with terror. But it doesn't . . . I guess I was half expecting it.* Aloud she said: 'Then you're quite a man.'

He relaxed again. 'That's what I told you. Men such as I are never defeated. Never destroyed. We may be pushed aside for a little time. But it does not matter. We wait. We are patient. We appear again.'

'But . . . how did you get in the Legion? I had an idea that men like you weren't allowed to enlist.'

'They are not. But I did not find it difficult. New papers, a new name . . . '

'So I guess you joined to get out of the way until things cooled off in Europe?'

'*Ja*. It is so. I have served for nearly ten years in this Legion. It has suited my purpose. In Germany people will have forgotten me. It will be safe at last for me to return. That, *fräulein*, is my reason for deserting!'

'Do — do the others know this? Hayle and Boroff, I mean.'

'They may guess. It does not matter. Now, *fräulein*, you must tell me . . . am I

110

not the one for you . . . ?'

Before she fully realised it, he had taken a couple of long strides. His great arms stretched out. They were round her waist. She felt like a fragile doll in the grasp of a fumbling giant.

She played her last card. She tilted back her head and forced herself to look once more straight at him. She parted her full lips into the semblance of a smile.

'Wait! Wait, Hermann! This is not the time . . . '

She was surprised to feel his grip relax. '*Ja*. You are right. First you must tell the American. Then he will know and there will be no trouble.'

She slipped out of his arms and moved swiftly to the other side of the tent. He did not attempt to follow her.

'When will you tell him?' he asked.

'Soon.'

'It must be now!'

'Tonight, then — now leave me.'

He watched her carefully, as a prospective purchaser might examine bloodstock. Then he crossed towards tent flap. Before leaving, he said: 'Don't try to trick me, *fräulein*. Remember — you will be mine whatever happens. But the life of Legionnaire Hayle depends on you!'

7

Caravan

Boroff woke. He cushioned his head on his arms and looked dreamily about the tent. He was surprised to see that Katz's bed was vacant, but relieved, too. Hayle was still sleeping.

Through the narrow aperture, Boroff watched the deep redness of the sinking sun. He thought about Katz. A flicker of fury burned in his meagre frame. God, how he hated Katz! And how he hated himself for being a coward!

At times such as this, when Katz was absent, he could see himself doing heroic things. Challenging the brute. Calling his bluff. Lashing him with biting phrases, while others looked on in wonder and admiration! If only such dreams could become reality . . .

But Boroff knew with clammy certainty that he was incapable of such greatness.

He was frozen by fear. Always had been. Fear had been his one permanent companion.

In Paris, when he was a boy, his main memory was of the fear in the eyes of his refugee parents as they talked of the Red Terror from which they had escaped. His bedtime stories had been blood-chilling descriptions of the unutterable cruelties man could inflict upon man.

That had been the foundation of dread. Then there had been the unbroken poverty. Living in a filthy tenement off Boul Diderot with the smell of the river coming in and the constant clang of trains in the Gare de Lyon. Would there be enough francs for food? Or to pay the rent? Or to get a pair of shoes repaired?

Fear. Always fear.

One of his many jobs had been the traditional one of driving a taxi. Because he had been afraid to cause offence, he lost many fares to more thrusting drivers. But once — just once — he had forced himself to quarrel with a particularly insulting competitor.

'*Mon ami*,' the French taxi driver had said, 'there only one way to settle this.'

Astounded at his own spirit, Boroff had agreed.

God! The pain of it! And the humiliation!

He had tried, but he could not get anywhere near the man. And a thousand iron fists seemed to be beating ceaselessly against his torn face. He was glad when he was knocked down. He pretended he could not get up. His opponent laughed at him and walked away. As the story spread, the others laughed, too. That was as bad as the beating itself.

It was then that Boroff knew finally that whatever happened, he must never challenge others. He could only lose. Only get hurt. And he feared pain.

During the Occupation, he had been invited to join the Resistance. He dared not. Later, it was hinted to him that he might profitably do donkey work for the Gestapo. He was afraid to do that, too. So he refused.

But there had been one solace. Alcohol. When he took enough of it, he felt big and strong. The stuff broke the shackles of the mind . . .

It was under the influence of vodka and tomato juice that he had gone to the Paris recruiting office and enlisted for five years in the Legion. Since then, his hell had become deeper and darker. Always he had been the target for the inevitable bully. And recently he had fallen under the heel of the worst bully of all — Hermann Katz.

He did not *want* to fawn on Katz! He loathed himself for doing it. But he had to. One look at Katz and the marrow shrivelled in his bones. He admired the American. Hayle was not afraid. But Boroff dared not show his admiration.

As he lay there, he wondered what Katz was doing. How long would it be before he heard the man bellowing for him?

He got off the camp bed and pulled on his boots. Then he went to the flap and peeped out.

Only the top half of the sun was showing. Soon it would be dark. To his left he saw a movement.

It was Katz, leaving the woman's tent

with a smile on his foul face! Boroff felt ill. He had scarcely spoken to her, but he liked her. The idea that she . . .

He saw something else. Something directly behind Katz and far beyond him. On the horizon. He screwed up his eyes. Camels!

There could be no doubt of it. They were not yet clearly defined, but he could identify the swaying movement. And they were approaching the oasis!

Boroff bobbed back into the tent. He kneeled beside Hayle and shook him.

'We're lucky!' he exclaimed when Hayle opened his eyes. 'A caravan's coming. A big one, I think.'

★   ★   ★

Among the retained stores was a pair of field-glasses. Katz looked through them, studying the Arabs. 'About forty camels,' he announced. 'Some mules, too.'

'Let me look.' Hayle took the glasses from him. He was pleasantly aware that Ruth was standing close beside him.

She asked: 'Will they stop here?'

'Sure to.'

'Then — then we'll be on our way?'

He lowered the glasses and shook his head. 'No, we won't. They're moving in the wrong direction. They'd take us away from the Spanish territory.'

He sensed her disappointment. Or was it more than that? He thought that just for a moment her entire body seemed to crumble. He said: 'Don't worry. There'll be others.'

Katz was restive, shuffling from one foot to another. He retrieved the glasses and looked through them again. Then he said decisively: 'We will have to take action, my friends!'

Hayle misunderstood the words. 'Oh, they'll be all right. They won't bother us. They'll only stay a night here and draw water. They'll have food.'

'I was not thinking of entertaining them!'

'What were you thinking of?'

'I was thinking that we will have to drive them off.'

Hayle regarded him incredulously. 'Drive them off! Why?'

'Because if we allow them to rest here, they may take our tents, even if they do not cut our throats. Do you not see that this is no ordinary caravan? It is a very big one. And when they know that there are only three men here, they may be tempted. I tell you, we must frighten them off — a few rounds of rapid fire and a glimpse of a uniform and they'll think a strong Legion column is here. It will be enough. But we must not let them guess how few of us there are!'

Hayle did not answer immediately. He was thinking fast. He had to admit that there was some truth in Katz's contention. This was obviously a long-distance caravan. As such, it would be well armed with tough, and probably not too scrupulous, Arab traders. It was not at all the sort of caravan they were hoping would take them towards the Spanish Sahara.

Therefore, it was at least possible that the Arabs, seeing obvious Legion deserters living in comparative comfort, would be inclined to take what they could see. True, most of the stores were hidden. But the luxury tents were themselves a worthwhile prize for men who were trekking great distances.

'We could fire over their heads,' Hayle said uncertainly. 'But I don't like the idea.'

'So! And why not?'

'They might need water urgently.'

'*Gott!* That is their worry! Do we have to make it ours?'

'And it'll do the Legion's reputation a lot of harm when it gets around that they're firing at caravans when they try to use an oasis.'

'The Legion's reputation! Does that concern us now? If you like the Legion so much, my friend, why do you want to leave it? I tell you — we must take up positions and give these Arabs a fright. A real fright, so they will not want to come here again for a long time.'

Hayle again took the glasses. They were now about two kilometres off and could be seen very clearly. There was no doubt that they were a tough-looking bunch, he thought.

He said: 'Okay. But remember — we're

not out to harm any of them. We just want to give them the idea that there's a whole lot of us and we don't like company. We'll have to take cover and spread out.'

They went back to the tents to get their Lebels.

Katz took up a position behind Ruth's tent, which was at the northern edge of the camp. Boroff had ensconced himself under the cover of the cluster of jaded palm trees. Hayle crouched in the excavation ditch. Ruth was with him. By implication, she had refused to leave his side. Katz had not said anything. There had not been time. But he glared a warning at her.

★   ★   ★

Despite his gathering years, Ata Masit's eyes remained sharp. Even when Lukka Oasis was far distant, he detected movement there. But he was unable even to guess how many people were in the place.

The knowledge annoyed him greatly. It

was evil fortune that others should have arrived before he. But he was still determined that what had been left there would be his. If the first arrivals chose to fight, then he would fight. But he hoped they would be sensible and leave the place in peace. He thought that they would almost certainly do so when they saw the strength of his caravan.

As the intervening distance narrowed, Masit became puzzled. The movement which he had noted earlier was now absent. There was not a sign of life in the oasis.

And darkness was approaching.

That was an extra annoyance, for Masit wanted to inspect the occupants of the oasis before entering it. He resolved to urge his camels to a trot, then halt within a stone's throw of the place.

He gave a hand signal. In single file, the caravan gathered pace and thundered towards Lukka. They were four hundred yards off and beginning to slacken pace when a series of rapid explosions came from the oasis. Simultaneously, there was a faint movement of air above their heads.

And an unnerving whine, like the faint whimper of an expiring animal. There was also the unmistakable closeness of death.

The caravan came to a slithering and confused stop. The drivers at the rear were having trouble with the mules, which had panicked and were kicking wildly.

Even as Masit was trying to assess the situation, another volley passed over their heads. Then a third.

He caught a glimpse of a kepi to his left. There was no mistaking it — a Legion kepi. There was another directly in front of him, among the palms. And further along, a smudge of uniform was discernible near a tent.

This was beyond all his calculations. Not only was the place occupied by a Legion force, but they were shooting at them!

In a reedy voice, Masit screamed an order. The caravan turned and retreated whence it came.

To himself, as he clung to his camel, Masit mouthed declarations of fury.

When the gathering darkness had

obscured them from view of the oasis, he halted his caravan. His *eflaheen* were shaken. But like Masit, they were conscious of rising wrath. They broke into an excited gabble — all declaiming, none listening.

It was some time before Masit could restore order. But when he did so, he showed the tenacious streak within him.

'The soldiers have come to see where the white men are slain,' he said, slowly. 'They shoot upon those who would disturb them. But I know how to get them away from this place so that we may seek the hidden coin.' He paused dramatically, then added: 'The soldiers will want to find those who did the slaying. I can aid them. I can tell them of my meeting with the Dylaks and of the course they have taken. When I have done that, the soldiers will be grateful to me. They will move out of the oasis to pursue the slayers. Thus, all of us will be satisfied.'

There was a mumble of admiration at their leader's shrewdness.

Masit waited for it to fade out. Then he

continued: 'The legionnaires will not shoot if only one of us approaches with the message and carries a sign of peace. I will do that. I will return to the oasis alone — now!'

* * *

Ruth said: 'Will they come back? We wouldn't see them now that it's dark.'

'I don't think there's any chance of that,' Hayle said. 'They're not real warriors, and they'll imagine that this place is packed with legionnaires.'

They had emerged from their firing positions and were clustered near the tents. Katz was triumphant. In the moonlight, his face shone with satisfaction.

'Was I not right?' he asked rhetorically. 'Was it not my plan to drive them off? And did it not work as I said it would?'

'Okay — so you're smart. But I hope those Arabs don't meet up with a caravan bound this way for Spanish territory. If they do, we might wait a long time for transport. I can't see many caravans waiting to call here if they know they're likely to be fired on.'

'*Nein!* You worry too much. The chances of such a meeting are very small — ' He broke off, as if the subject no longer interested him. He looked at Ruth. She was standing close to Hayle. She had never left him in the last two hours.

Katz said very slowly, pronouncing each word with care: 'Now . . . my little *fräulein*! Have you spoken to our friend yet? Shall I leave you while you do that? It will be the last time I will leave you . . . '

Hayle was blowing sand from the bolt mechanism of his rifle. He stopped doing so abruptly. Puzzled, he looked first at Ruth, then at Katz.

'What's this? What are you talking about, Katz?'

Katz gave smile of a contented man. 'She will tell you.'

'Leave her out of it! You tell me!'

'*Nein.* I said that she will tell you, my friend, and that is how it will be . . . you want to tell him, don't you, *fräulein*?'

She turned away from him. A tremor of

126

shivering took hold of her body. She fought hard to control it, but could not.

Hayle put a hand on her elbow. He stared hard at her. 'What's the matter? Has he been bothering you?'

She did not answer. She seemed to look through him rather than at him. For in that moment she was not seeing him as he was, standing there. She saw him on his tent bed, a slash in his neck where a bayonet had been inserted. Or a big oozing wound where a hot and cruel bullet had entered, done while he slept. When he was helpless, as all men are helpless at such times . . .

How long since she had met him? Twenty-four hours. No more. Yet she *knew* him. Knew him better than any man. In an awkward, embarrassed way, he had stripped bare his heart to her when he had spoken to her in the tent. Eddie Hayle from Wichita, Kansas. Her own home State.

Was he very different from millions of other young Americans? No. He was brave and nervous. He tried to conceal his nerves under the traditional crust of cynicism, just as he attempted to hide kindness and generosity. But she was not deceived. No woman would be deceived.

Now, way back in the States, another woman was ill. Hoping to see him. Telling herself she *would* see him.

He would reach her. Eddie Hayle was the sort of man who would conquer the challenge of deserts and seas. If he was not murdered by a bestial thug in his sleep . . .

So what did it come to? It was simple, really. Just a matter of who was the most important between two young American citizens. Eddie Hayle or Ruth Westlake.

Well, what did she herself have that made living so important? Nothing. Now her father was dead, there was no family. There had been her work. As her father's secretary, she had found a deep fascination in following the course of lost civilisations and forgotten peoples. But she would not find it so fascinating now.

Eddie was the one who mattered. She was the threat to his life. If they had not found her, there would never have been this crisis.

She felt a pain in her arm. It was Eddie, gripping her elbow tight. He was repeating the question.

'What's the matter?'

Now was the time. No further delay. But Katz had to be stalled just a little longer, while she looked for her father's pistol which she knew was still in the tent.

She snatched her arm away. Her eyes became hard, her voice harsh. 'Keep your hands off me!'

'But I — '

'Can't you see what the setup is? If you can't, you're dumb! I want to get out of this mess alive!'

'But of course you do! And you will. There's no need to get mad about it.'

'I'm not mad! It's just that a little while ago I came to my senses. I had a talk with Katz. Yes, with Katz! I began thinking then that he was the right sort of man to look after a woman in a mess like this. He's got something about him. And when I saw how he handled those Arabs, I knew I was right! So get this — if I have to string along with anyone here, it'll be Katz!'

Hayle did not move. His hand remained half extended, a position it had assumed after she had pulled away. Deep shadows seemed to gather suddenly under his eyes. He looked old.

He said gently: 'You're sure you know what you're doing, Ruth?'

'I know.'

Katz moved up to her. He put a heavy arm round her shoulders. She tensed. But she did not resist. Katz was smiling deeply now. His lips were stretched wide. He glistened with triumph.

'You are sensible, *fräulein*! It is true that I will look after you well. Now let us — '

'Just a minute!'

Hayle's voice cut in sharply. Katz regarded him with something approaching benevolent tolerance. '*Ja*. What is it?'

But Hayle was not looking at him. He was addressing Ruth. 'I don't believe you,' he said. 'Right now, I can't figure exactly what's happened. But I don't believe you ever had a talk with Katz. I've never left Katz since we found you.'

Boroff moved excitedly forward. This

was his moment. 'Katz has been with her,' he announced eagerly. 'Katz does not tell lies! I saw him come out of her tent just before the caravan was sighted. He looked so very pleased. I thought this would happen!'

His brief period of importance over, Boroff retreated back to the shadows. He was fearful now in case he had said too much. Something which would displease Katz.

Hayle glanced towards the Russian. Then he shook his head, as if trying to collect a fragment of reality out of a nightmare.

He said: 'Ruth . . . you've got to forget that Katz is here. You must realise there's no need to be scared of him. I can handle him, if I have to. Now tell me — have you said this because you wanted to? Or is it because he frightened you into it?'

Her pale throat twitched. That was her only sign of emotion. Her voice was still hard as she said: 'You heard me right the first time. I've been around and I know what I'm doing. I figure the man to look after me is Katz. I'm throwing in with him.'

'I don't know for sure what you mean when you talk about throwing in with him, Ruth. But I can make a guess. And it doesn't please me any. Understand this — you don't have to throw in with any guy here. Not Katz, not me, not Boroff. We'll all see you okay as far as the United States consulate at Villa Cisneros. And that's as far as it needs to go. You've only got to say the word and it's as far as it will go.'

'Quit making speeches. I find them tedious!'

'I don't think you do, Ruth. You know that what I'm saying is right. You're not the kind of woman to throw herself at a degraded, blustering oaf like Katz! Anyway, not willingly. The Legion's a pretty tough outfit, and a lot of the guys in it aren't all they ought to be. But there's not many of them who thought much of Katz. He's just a bad little bum with a big body and a loud voice!'

Katz gave a roar. A pure animal roar. The satisfaction had been fading from his face. Now he had reached a state of fury verging on madness.

He pushed Ruth out of the way. She stumbled and fell. Then, like a goaded bear, he rushed at Hayle.

Ruth was glad that they were fighting. It gave her the opportunity she wanted. A few minutes was all she needed to find that pistol. Then there would be no woman for them to quarrel about.

Katz charged with his head down. For a man of his bulk, he could move with astonishing speed. Hayle waited until he was almost on him, then he sidestepped. But he mistimed it. The German's head crashed against his right thighbone. He was knocked off balance and hit the ground as Katz swept past.

It was as he sprawled on the ground that Hayle realised he was still holding his Lebel. The breech was empty, but used as a club it would be a decisive weapon. He had a strong momentary desire to use it. In the same circumstances, Katz would have done. But Katz had given his rifle to Boroff to carry. He was unarmed. So that was the way it had to be for both of them.

Hayle left his gun on the ground as he scrambled to his feet. He was only just in time to brace himself for Katz's next charge. But this time the German was more orthodox. He had lost his initial wildness and was using his brain. He came in fast, but only slightly crouched and with left fist extended. It was an ungainly but fairly orthodox fighting approach.

This time Hayle felt more confident. While in the Air Corps, he had done a lot of boxing. He was sure that if he waited for the right moment, he would be able to nail Katz in a slugging match.

Katz did not complete his attack. He stopped suddenly, just short of Hayle, as if realising that he was not confronting a novice. The two circled each other slowly, waiting for an opening.

Hayle gave a tight smile. He hissed between his teeth: 'Come on, Katz. Why're you dancing around? Are you scared of getting hurt?'

It was a deliberate attempt to spur the German into again losing his temper. Hayle knew well enough that his best chance of finishing the struggle early was to tempt Katz into making a wild attack.

He succeeded.

Katz made a cumbersome leap forward and swung viciously with his right. It was a punch which, if it had landed, would have knocked any man unconscious. But no one skilled in ringcraft could possibly have been caught by it, for it was a lead with the wrong hand. Before being delivered, the elbow was pulled well back, thus giving warning. And it moved through the air in an almost complete semi-circle.

It was an open invitation to a right-counter. Hayle accepted it.

While the punch was travelling, Hayle took a very short forward step. This brought him safely inside the orbit of the fist. Then he unleashed his own right hand at Katz's fleshy chin.

He felt a brief, jarring pain flash down his forearm. He saw Katz's head jerk back as though on a hinge. Then the German was rolling on the ground.

Hayle relaxed. It was an automatic reaction to what he felt certain was a knock-out punch. But in that respect he had underestimated Katz. The immensely tough German was dazed, but no more.

Katz rolled on to his knees. He held his head down and shook it. He was breathing noisily.

Hayle asked: 'Have you taken enough, Katz? If you have, maybe we can start talking. I want to get a few things cleared up around here.'

Katz did not answer. Not verbally. He swivelled round on his knees and flung his arms round Hayle's ankles. There was no possibility of keeping balance. Hayle fell.

But he remembered to relax his legs so as to reduce the impact. Even so, his forehead struck the ground violently. And fragments of sand got into his eyes. He was compelled to screw his lids closed and to rub them with his knuckles. For the moment he was blind. Helpless.

Katz saw the rifle. He grunted in satisfaction as he stumbled to it. He cocked the firing pin and raised it to take precise aim at Hayle's head.

* * *

Ruth found the revolver. It was at the bottom of her father's carrying bag, secreted between spare shirts. With unfamiliar fingers, she spun the chamber. It was empty. She groped again among the clothing, searching frantically for ammunition. Above all things, she wanted to carry through her decision before she became too frightened to do so. After a few seconds, she uncovered a small cartoon of cartridges.

She carried both the gun and the carton to a chair and sat down. Now to load the weapon. Now to end this awful hell.

But how did one load a Colt revolver? She had a vague idea that the spinning chamber could be released so that it hung free of the hammer and butt. Then there would be space to press a cartridge into place.

Her fingers fumbled for a release catch. But she was not mechanically minded. And she had practically no knowledge of firearms.

Instinct warned her that the fight could not last long. When two such big men clashed, it would certainly end quickly. Fearfully, her fingers still vainly manipulating, she glanced outside.

They were only shadows. But she knew it was Katz who held the rifle. His back was to her, and those vast shoulders could belong to no other. And it was Eddie who was on the ground, rubbing for some reason at his face.

She was not aware of making a decision. Not aware, even, of moving. But suddenly she was out of the tent and running towards them. When she was fifteen yards from Katz, she stopped.

Ruth screamed: 'Drop that rifle . . . or I'll shoot!'

And she aimed the empty Colt at him.

★   ★   ★

Ata Masit was astonished. It seemed that all his caution was for nought.

He had approached the oasis alone, obviously unarmed, and holding aloft between his gnarled hands a square of white material which he understood to be an acceptable token of peace.

As he got within sight of the place, he had expected to be challenged by Legion sentries. No challenge came. He thought that perhaps they were watching him from points of concealment and would surround him when he drew level with the cluster of palms. No such thing happened.

Gradually, it became born upon Masit that the oasis was not strongly held by legionnaires. In fact, as he stood near the well, he wondered whether any soldiers were now there at all.

Then he heard a woman shouting. A wild and brief series of words. He looked in their direction. He counted four silhouettes.

His sense of prudence battled with his innate curiosity. His curiosity won. Masit moved towards those silhouettes.

★　★　★

Hayle managed to open his stinging eyes as he heard Ruth's voice. They were streaming moisture, and they showed the shadows around him as though through a bent mirror. He rubbed them again as he staggered upright. Now his vision became clear.

Katz had turned. He was facing Ruth.

And Katz was saying: 'Leave these matters to me, *fräulein*! You must learn to obey.'

'Drop that rifle!' She waved the revolver. Katz smiled.

'You are too far away, *fräulein*! You could not shoot me from there. If you think you can use that gun, then come closer.'

'If I have to, I can manage from here. I'm a good shot.'

She did not speak as if she was a good shot. There was a note of vibrant uncertainty in her voice. Katz did not miss it. He laughed.

He was still laughing when Hayle, moving quietly up from the rear, slashed the edge of his palm onto the back of Katz's neck.

The point of impact was at the nerve centre immediately below the base of the skull. The result was a temporary paralysis of all Katz's motor nerves. He folded rather than fell to the ground.

If Hayle had delivered the blow with greater force, it would have killed Katz. As it was, it caused him brief agony and a vomiting bout.

But Hayle did not concern himself further with him. He ran towards Ruth and took the gun from her hand. She not attempt to resist. He glanced at it and noted the empty chamber. Then he saw the carton of cartridges which she was still clutching.

'Thanks,' he said. 'That was fast thinking, Ruth. I'm glad you decided to bluff it out. If you'd waited to load this thing, you'd have been too late.'

He thrust the revolver into his belt. Then he held her shoulders. He added in a whisper: 'You've got what it takes! I guess there aren't many women who'd take that kind of risk to save a guy.'

She did not answer. She wanted to feel the physical certainty of his protection. But she could not. He did not know why she happened to have that gun in her hand. He must not know. But she must get the gun back. It was still needed — nothing had really changed.

Ruth said harshly: 'You can cut out! Maybe I didn't want to see you murdered. I've seen enough. But I didn't want to see Katz with a price on his head, either. I'm relying on Katz!'

'Look, I . . . '

Someone coughed. The sound came from a few paces away. It had an unfamiliar tone. They turned, and suddenly became very still. The figure of an Arab was standing there. He clutched a piece of white material. He was elderly, almost old. But in his bearded face there was alertness and cunning.

The Arab said: 'I am Ata Masit, leader of a caravan bound for the Niger River. I come in peace.'

He spoke in a form of French peculiar to his people. But there was a sense of dignity in it.

Hayle recovered from the worst of his astonishment. 'You mean . . . you have the caravan we . . . '

'It is so. Mine is the caravan you fired

upon. We sought no harm and I do not understand.'

Hayle ignored the implied question. 'Are you alone?'

Masit slowly nodded.

'What do you want here?'

'I wish to speak with the officer of your patrol.'

Hayle was about to deny the existence of such a person. But sudden caution deterred him. 'You can say anything you want to me. I'll take a message. But you'd no right to come here, Masit. This . . . this place is under military occupation.'

It was a weak, unconvincing statement. Masit dealt with it by making a broad gesture. 'Then where are the soldiers? I can see but three! And no sentries stand guard!'

He was looking around him. His covetous eyes embraced the tents. Then they switched eagerly towards the site of the excavations.

Katz approached. His eyes were glazed and his fleshy face hung slack. He was rubbing the back of his neck. But he had heard the exchanges. Katz stared ferociously at the Arab.

'What do you want? Answer — or I'll beat your tongue loose!'

Masit regarded Katz coldly. The Arab was obviously feeling increasingly confident. Three legionnaires and woman could offer no opposition to his men. And coin might be there for the taking . . .

Masit said: 'I was surprised that the Legion should shoot at us, for the days of such warfare are done. But now I know that it did not happen — for three deserters and a woman are not a Legion patrol. Yes, I can see with my eyes and my heart that you are fleeing from your ow soldiers. But that would not have concerned me if you had chosen to receive us in peace. Yet you tried to slay us, so I feel a great wrath.'

Katz flourished a fist under Mask's bearded chin. 'Swine. We did not try to kill you! *Nein!* But we do not want you here — understand?'

Masit was unperturbed. He looked reflectively at Katz. 'Is it that you also seek the coins which are buried?'

'Coins! What are you snivelling about?'

'Do not look so surprised, big legionnaire! Have you not guessed that I know of the slaughter in this place?'

Hayle said: 'So that's why your caravan came here! You want to finish the looting.'

Masit shrugged. He did not bother to answer. There followed several uncertain moments. Then Katz turned his back on Masit and faced Hayle.

'*Gott!* Do you see what this means?' Katz asked.

'I guess so. It means that when the rest of the Arabs come here, they'll probably knife us.'

'*Ja.* Or hand us back to the Legion and ask for a reward.'

A further silence. Masit regarded them contemptuously, almost suavely.

Ruth had been standing slightly in the background, white and trembling. But she had followed every word. She said unexpectedly, so that they all turned to stare at her: 'There's only one answer, isn't there?'

Hayle had a notion of what was in her mind. But he said: 'Okay, let's have it.'

'Let me get one thing straight first — is this Arab in charge of the caravan?'

Masit apparently understood her, for he inclined his head and said: 'It is my caravan. I have forty servants with me, but I alone can guide it to the Niger. My word is the law, and if you wish to plead with me I will hear you.'

She ignored the insult. But she looked triumphantly at Hayle. 'That's what I hoped! We'll have to keep him here as a hostage.'

Katz grasped the point immediately. He expanded on it. 'That is good, my *fräulein*! We must let the Arabs know that Masit will be safe if they keep out of the way. But if they try to approach this place, we'll kill him. If he's as important as he says he is, they won't want to lose him.'

It was a savage solution. Hayle felt a natural repugnance towards it. But it was the one barrier they could raise in their defence. Simultaneously, all of them turned again towards Masit.

The Arab had lost his composure. He was uncertain — obviously wanting to attempt an escape, but fearing the consequences if he did.

Katz was by now almost fully recovered from the blow on his neck. This was a situation in which he was an expert. He was eager to demonstrate his skill. He gripped Masit's wrist. With a flicking movement, he twisted the Arab's scrawny arm behind his back. Masit groaned as his tendons stretched. He lost balance, but quickly recovered it as his own weight added to the pain. Katz was smiling. Hayle had seen him smile many times before. But he noticed that this was the first occasion in which there was any genuine humour in it. Katz had forgotten all else in his unadulterated enjoyment of the situation.

He asked: 'Will your men hear you if you shout?'

Masit nodded wildly, showing the off-whites of his eyes.

'That is good! Now, my friend, you will call to them to come just a little closer. Just close enough for them to hear every word. Then you will tell them to keep out of here — or you will die.'

8

Casualties

Corporal Jurgan said: 'With respect, *mon officier*, I think we will have to leave them.'

For a moment, Lieutenant Garnia was silent. Then he gestured to the seat he had shaped out of the sand. 'Sit down, corporal.'

Jurgan sat. Despite his exhaustion, he contrived to beam his pleasure at the honour accorded him.

Garnia murmured: 'You are right, of course. It has been cruel to bring them even this far. But what else could I do?' He cupped his chin in his hands and gazed up at the stars, brooding about the five legionnaires. Five without equipment, tunics or boots.

Or boots . . .

That was the essence of the trouble. Several legionnaires had tried to assist the unfortunate five by tearing great lengths off their *bougerons*, which were wrapped round their feet. But linen was a poor substitute for proper footwear. Sand worked through. And soon the men were limping. This had slowed the whole column during the day. Just before the halt at nightfall, the bootless ones were almost being carried by their comrades.

Because his charts were burned and he lacked a compass, Garnia could only make a rough assessment of their position. But he knew that if they continued at the present nightmare pace, they would in all probability die of thirst. For their meagre water supplies, even on the basis of a few sips every two hours, could not last more than another day. Therefore, the five must be left here while the others pushed forward as fast as possible.

There would certainly be spare clothing at the oasis. Some of this would be borrowed from the archaeological expedition. And with a few volunteers, he would return with it to bring back the five. He did not like leaving the men. But the alternative was death for all of them.

Garnia stood up abruptly. Jurgan followed. 'We will march again in ten minutes,' Garnia said.

Jurgan's eyebrows shot up. 'Ten minutes, *mon officier*! But I thought we were bivouaced for the night.'

'We were, but I have changed my mind. If we start now, we ought to reach Lukka Oasis before midday. The expedition there will have mules. We will use those to return immediately and retrieve the lame ones. If all goes well, we will all be together at the oasis by this time tomorrow.'

Jurgan said diffidently: 'The men are tired. They had no sleep last night.'

'I know it. I am tired, too. But I'd rather go short of sleep than short of water. I'll give the order to strike camp — but first I want to speak with the men we are leaving here.'

The legionnaires were huddled in a circle. Although it was less than an hour since they had halted, a few were already sleeping. But most were awake, their blankets round their shoulders. The inevitable pack of cards had appeared and some were playing, straining their eyes at the pasteboards under the moonlight. Garnia had deemed it unnecessary to mount a guard. No one knew they were there, and in any case he knew of no hostility towards them.

Garnia picked his way towards the casualties. As fellow sufferers, they had grouped together. All of them had removed the tattered linen from their feet. They were regarding their extremities with morbid interest. Garnia looked at them, too. They confirmed the correctness of his decision.

The soles of their feet were lacerated horribly and sand had caked into the wounds. Unless they received a medical dressing soon, there was a certainty of infection. The men could not march — or limp — much further.

Garnia sat beside them. The five watched him curiously. They recognised the friendly gesture. But like all soldiers, they were immediately suspicious of the officer who made it.

'*Tiens!* Your feet look bad!' Garnia

151

said. 'You have done very well to get this far. Very well, indeed. But you will not have to do any more walking. I am leaving you here while the rest of us push on immediately. We will be back for you by tomorrow evening. Perhaps well before that. You will only have to wait twenty-four hours at the most.'

Their suspicion changed to astonishment. One of them, an Argentinian who was quick to see any potential injustice, said quickly: 'But we can't survive twenty-four hours, *mon officier*. We have lost everything — we have no food, water or rifles.'

'You have shared food and water thus far,' Garnia said crisply. 'You will go on sharing it. Enough will be left for you.'

'But suppose you do not come back . . . '

'*Dieu!* Do you think I would leave you here to rot? Be careful what you say, legionnaire!'

The Argentinian was silent for a few seconds. But he was not abashed. He said: 'We are unarmed.'

'What of it?'

'It is not good to be defenceless in such a place as this.'

Garnia had to admit the truth of the claim. There was little prospect of anyone finding them during the short period they would be alone, but there was always the off-chance that a group of itinerant Arabs would come this way. And they might be tempted to interfere with five unarmed and crippled legionnaires. Certainly, the days of large-scale anti-French activities were gone. But Garnia had in mind that there had recently been a revival of fierce Arab nationalism. This had been largely fostered in the towns, and it was the result of foreign political propaganda. But it had shown signs of spreading to the remote areas. Therefore, under such conditions, it would be unfair to leave the men without means of defence.

'You will each be given a rifle,' he said. Then, to end the discussion, he rose and gave the order to form a column.

As he did so, he was aware of a mounting sense of worry. His strength was about to be reduced to twenty-four men. And since five of them were about to surrender their rifles, only nineteen would be armed.

He tried to reassure himself. *Why should I bother?* he thought. *I'm not due for any more trouble. We are going to an oasis where a friendly party of American scientists will welcome us!*

But that hard lump had returned within his belly. His nerves were strained again, quivering like a plucked violin string. He was feeling just as he had done back in Post D. It was a return of the premonition. The same sort of premonition that had warned him of the fire . . .

9

Rescue

They had heard the voice of Masit.

First, they had heard it faintly, calling to them from the edge of the oasis and bidding them come a little closer. The men of the caravan had done so. And they had listened in alarm as their leader told of his duress and theirs.

But the alarm had quickly changed to wrath when they moved back to their camp to talk.

They were no fools, the *felaheen* of Masit's caravan. As they discussed his message, they reached a surprisingly accurate assessment of the situation in the oasis.

Masit had said: 'I am held by three legionnaires who will slay me if you do not leave this place.'

Only three! Then, obviously, they must be deserters. They must be very frightened deserters, too. Being afraid, they would spend the night huddled together, guarding their prisoner.

It would be easy for *felaheen* such as they, naturally skilled in stealth, to penetrate the oasis without being seen or heard. The Arabs fingered their knives thoughtfully. They believed that even if they withdrew, Masit would probably be killed. So they could do no harm by attempting a rescue. And if all else failed, they would slay the legionnaires. Thus, honour would be satisfied.

*　*　*

Ruth said: 'Would you give me back the revolver?'

Hayle looked at the weapon in his belt. Then at her. 'Well . . . do you know how to use it? These things can be mighty dangerous if you don't.'

'Of course I do,' she lied.

'Then let me see you load it. You've got a carton of slugs in your hand.'

They were standing in the main tent. Masit, hands and legs lashed together, was sprawled on the ground. Katz was

156

opening cans of food while Boroff was lighting a spirit stove.

'Go on, Ruth — load it!'

He handed the gun to her. He watched her fumbling, slightly desperate efforts. Then he smiled and took it from her.

'Maybe you won't do yourself any harm with that — but you won't do any good, either. I'd better keep it. What do you want it for, anyway?'

'Any woman would want a gun when she's alone with three men, wouldn't she? I want it for self-protection, that's all.'

She was a bad liar. The explanation was reasonable enough, but it did not ring true.

'You've got your self-protection. You chose him yourself, remember? He's there, working on the cans. His name's Katz.'

She moistened her lips. 'That still leaves two of you ... Katz can't be around all the time! I want ... '

'Cut it out, Ruth! You're not kidding me anymore! You don't look like a tramp. You can't even talk like a tramp! I don't believe you want to hook up with Katz for

157

self-protection. I figure there's another reason, and I'm going to find out what it is.'

She glanced towards Katz. A scared glance. He was holding an empty can in hand, the jagged lid half raised. He took a heavy step towards her. He was watching her.

Hayle continued: 'I can guess that Katz has scared you in some way. If you won't tell me what he said, maybe Katz himself will.'

Hayle turned towards Katz. The German was balancing the can base down in his right palm. He continued to stare at Ruth. She tried to meet his gaze. For a few moments she succeeded. Then she had to turn away.

'You've scared the daylights out of her, Katz. I want to know what you've said.'

'I have said nothing — except to tell her that she's safest with a man such as I.'

The skin round Hayle's jaw tightened. He said very quietly: 'One of us two has got to die . . . that's right, isn't it, Katz? And you figure it's going to be me.'

Katz raised his eyebrows. 'I did not say

so! I think we can get along very well . . . if you are sensible and don't concern yourself too much with this woman.'

'But I *am* concerning myself with her, and it's going to stay that way. I don't care what she says or what you say — but you're not going to put a hand on her! D'you get it?'

Katz's hand tightened round the open can. 'You're a fool! A big fool! Now listen to me — you want to get back to America, don't you? You have told me why. Then think, Hayle! Think hard! If we fight any more, I might win. I might kill you. But there's someone in America hoping to see you before she dies. Do want her to be disappointed because you chose to be heroic over this *fräulein*? You are wrong when you say one must go. Both of us can live — if you are sensible!'

Ruth gave a peculiar whimper. She looked pleadingly at Hayle. 'Eddie . . . '

'Oh, so I'm 'Eddie' again!'

'Please . . . what Katz says is right! You're the most important person here. You've got the best reason for living. A decent, human reason. Don't you see you've got to play it Katz's way? We all have to, or he'll . . . '

She broke off suddenly, realising that she had too much. But Hayle caught the significance. Suddenly he was almost shouting.

'Go on, Ruth! Don't stop there — I want to know the rest. What will Katz do? *Tell me!*'

She backed away from him, found a chair, and slumped into it. She sat with her head over her chest, sobbing.

Katz said: 'I think I will tell you, Hayle. Since she has told you so much, I might as well give you the rest.'

'Go on, Katz. I'm listening.'

'She has agreed to let me — er — adopt her. But you are right in thinking there is a very personal reason. You see — I told her that if she refused, you might die in your sleep!'

'I might . . . '

'*Ja!* Men can have accidents in their sleep.'

Ruth stopped sobbing. The only sound was the breathing of the two men.

Then Hayle whispered: 'Have you

160

thought that you could have the same sort of accident, Katz?'

He nodded. '*Ja!* But you would not be the cause of it, my friend. You would not kill a man while he slept, would you?'

'I could kill you right now.'

'You could try. But it would be a big risk. Supposing you failed?'

'I could take that chance.'

'It seems a big risk to take when you are well on the way to returning to America. Listen, Hayle — I will quarrel with you no more. I will not provoke you. I will never start a fight. You will have no excuse to get rid of me. But if you try to come between me and the woman . . . then I will knife you when you can do nothing to defend yourself. So ask yourself this question — which means the most to you, the *fräulein* or your mother who is ill in America? Think about it carefully. When you have done so, I believe you will hold your peace.'

Hayle heard the harsh voice as if from far off. But the merciless challenge was clear.

The cable was still in his tunic. The

cable from Wichita. It had driven him nearly crazy when he had received it. Such a message would have done the same to most men.

Now what was it that suddenly came between him and his home that he must reach? He tried to answer the question calmly, stripping it of all sentiment.

It was a woman. What sort of woman? She was young. But there was no particular virtue about that, he reminded himself. Youth was merely the decaying foundation of old age. She was beautiful. But there was nothing very exceptional about that. Beauty was a fairly well distributed feminine asset. By coincidence she was also an American. There were one hundred and forty-six million other Americans.

So what? Why should he worry about her?

Fallen in love? Hell, no!

Then what was there about her which made her so important?

It was because he, Eddie Hayle, was important to *her*!

She wanted him to live. Wanted it so

much that she was even ready to sacrifice herself to Katz. Just to make sure of his safety. That sort of thing didn't happen very often to a person. Maybe that sort of woman wasn't around so very much.

Eddie Hayle decided.

He decided that the chances might be against him ever seeing Wichita again. Probably he'd be murdered in the Algerian desert instead.

Suddenly the problem cleared. He had a hunch that if his mother knew all the awful facts, she'd understand . . .

Katz was talking again. 'So you will leave us alone my friend . . . I and the *fräulein?*'

'No!'

'Ah — ! You know the price you will pay?'

'I may pay it. Or I may not. But I'm not going to wait for you to knife me in my sleep, Katz. I'm going to kill you — now!'

'I'm not holding a gun. Will you shoot an unarmed man?'

'Your Lebel's on the floor, Katz. So is mine. Let's see who's the fastest.'

'*Nein*. I will make no attempt to pick it up.'

Hayle thought: *I'd be justified in killing him, anyway. But I can't do it! I can't shoot a man who won't shoot back! And Katz knows it!*

Aloud, Hayle said: 'If you don't like shooting, let's see what we can do with our bare hands.'

Katz did not answer verbally. He thrust his hands into the pockets of his slacks. Then he turned his back. The can fell to the ground.

Hayle grasped his shoulders. With an effort, he swivelled the German towards him. Then standing back, he poised himself for a punch. He unleashed a vicious right jab into the centre of Katz's stomach. There was plenty of warning, but Katz made no attempt to avoid the blow. His hands were still in his pockets as he grunted and fell sideways, rolling on the trussed figure of Masit. He lay there for a full minute, retching slightly. When he got up, he swayed.

He said: 'Hit me again, my friend! I will

164

not strike back — yet. I can afford to wait.'

Frantically, Hayle probed for some way of provoking him into a defence. If only Katz would defend himself, then he could try to kill him.

Hayle chanced to glance at Masit. The Arab was on his side, looking up at them in bewilderment and fear. He was grunting, too, for he had suffered some pain when Katz's great weight descended on him. But Hayle was not concerned at this moment with Masit's welfare. He was concentrating on the ropes which bound the Arab.

There was the answer! No need to try to kill Katz! There was a simple solution. He must take advantage of this situation to knock Katz unconscious with a hook to the jaw. Then he must tie him up — just as Masit was tied.

Katz could be kept like that until a caravan came which would take them into Spanish territory. After that, Katz would not be able to do much harm, for it would not be difficult to enlist the support of the Arabs against him if necessary.

Easy! Why hadn't he thought of it before?

*   *   *

Masit's *felaheen* moved with the smooth silence of shadows.

First they formed a rough circle outside the area of the tents. Then they began to close in. They crawled. Knives were gripped in their teeth. And they converged on the big tent.

When they were less than twenty yards from it, they rose. It was like the manifestation of forty evil spirits.

*   *   *

Hayle pulled back his fist. He balanced himself carefully. There must be no mistake. This must be a knockout punch, for Katz would certainly drop his attitude of no resistance if he knew he was being bound.

Katz waited for it, hands still in his pockets. His eye were mere slits. A nerve in his bull-like neck pulsated. Those were his only signs of emotion.

Hayle thought: *Damn you! But you've got guts!*

His fist was only partially closed — he would not snap it shut until the moment of impact. Hayle knew that a tightly clenched hand does not travel as fast as one which is relaxed. He prepared to roll his body weight with the blow.

Something seized his arms. Before he realised it, they were dragged behind his back.

The next moment, the tent seemed to be congested with Arabs.

Several of them were round Katz, holding curved blades to his stomach. Others were holding Boroff and Ruth. And one of them was slashing through the ropes which held Masit.

★   ★   ★

Masit was helped to a chair. One of his *felaheen* gave him water. The old Arab was shaken, but his mind was clear again. He held up a restraining hand when his men demanded permission to deal with the legionnaires and the woman.

'They will die,' he announced. 'Even the woman will die. But it will be slow, so that the vengeance shall linger. The time is not now, for we are weary. It will be in the morning, when we are rested.'

Katz spat hard. 'You're a fool, Masit! If you kill us, the French will find you, and — '

'I do not think the French will worry about the deaths of three deserters,' Masit interrupted gently.

Katz attempted a weak lie. 'We are not deserters. We are an advance patrol. Others are coming.'

Almost sympathetically, Masit shook his head.

'You forget that I heard you talk of your plans to escape. But understand this — we will not slay you because you are legionnaires. It will be because you fired at us when we came in peace, then you were prepared to kill me to keep my men away.'

As he listened, Hayle felt compelled to admit that the Arab's decision contained a grim logic. He said urgently: 'Whatever you choose to do with us can be prevented. And you're right when you say the French won't bother about us. But Ruth — that's different. She was a member of the expedition. She's the only survivor. And she had nothing to do with what's happened here. You've got to spare her — got to!'

Masit looked at Ruth with new interest. He asked: 'Is this true? Were you in the expedition?'

'I was. And — '

'The Dylaks told me that all had died, but they were ever great boasters. Yet it does not matter, for I know they did not boast about the coins, for I saw them, and I believe there may be others amid the ruins.'

Ruth was being loosely held by two Arabs. She jerked her hands free from them. Watching her, Hayle caught a transitory flicker of hope on her face. She said: 'Is that what you want — more coins?'

'We will search and hope.'

'But you'll never find them. Oh yes, they're there. They must be. My father said there were others. But you could dig for years and not see even one, because you don't know where to look.'

She spoke with conviction. Masit was obviously impressed.

'And do you know?'

'I do.'

'Then you will show us — and we may spare your life.'

'I'll show you, if you spare all of us.'

'Only you. I will make that bond and no more.'

'Then you'll learn nothing from me!'

'You could be persuaded . . .'

'You mean you'd torture me?'

'We would.'

Ruth licked her lips, but her blue eyes were hard. They fixed themselves on Masit. She said: 'Look at me! Do you think I'd break? You're wrong! Spare all of us, and I'll help you. Those are my terms.'

Masit considered carefully. He was a fair judge of character, this old Arab. He had a shrewd notion that this white woman would not be an easy subject for coercion. On the other hand, the money interested him vastly. It interested all of them. He decided to accept her offer — on a condition.

He asked: 'Will it take long to find the coins?'

'I don't know. A day, maybe more.'

'Then let us hope that it is no more than a day. We will start digging under your directions in the morning. If the coins are not found by sundown, all of you will die. I am sorry I have to make such a condition, but we cannot afford to stay here too long.'

He rose, and clutching his *burnous* around a scraggy frame with a slightly pathetic attempt at dignity, the aged, crafty and avaricious Masit swept out of the tent.

★ ★ ★

They were left in that tent. All four of them.

Their hands and feet were lashed behind their backs — for Masit had given orders that they were to be secured in exactly the same way that he himself had been. They were in the nominal custody of one Arab guard. It was nominal because the man, understandably weary, lay back in one of the chairs, dozing. He gave only an occasional glance at his charges on the ground, and these became less frequent. The man could be excused for such apparent neglect of duty. There was no chance of the prisoners escaping. The ropes which tied them were knotted by men who were experts in the craft. There was no possibility of working them loose.

Hayle was watching the Arab guard. He had been doing so for more than an hour. He was also showing some interest in a food can which lay three feet from him. An open can, its jagged lid raised . . .

He looked at the three others. Ruth was against the opposite wall of the tent. She looked like a child. Her blonde head was resting on a small box, and her hair was tousled round her shoulders. She was sleeping fitfully, occasionally moving her lips as if to mumble a word. It would be risky trying to reach her. She was too far away.

Next, Hayle studied Katz. The German

was not asleep, but neither was he awake. As he lay on his side — the only feasible position for all of them — his half-closed eyes occasionally twitched. His lips were pursed and very faintly he seemed to be whistling a marching tune, something with an emphatic beat. Probably Katz was dreaming of his glories past and anticipating similar ones to come.

Hayle thought that on the whole, Katz was the best partner for his plan. But he, too, was some distance away. And he was fairly near the guard.

Boroff . . .

The little Russian was contriving to wipe tear stains off his thin face with his shoulders. Boroff had had enough. He had endured experiences such as would break stronger men than he. Now the last fragment of courage had drained from his heart. He had been enjoying a quiet weep. Each generous tear symbolised Boroff's deep pity for himself and his sorrow for the cruelties of the world.

Hayle regarded him analytically. Previously he had felt no emotion towards Boroff other than occasional moments of sympathy. But now he was trying to assess his usefulness. He was a mere five feet from Hayle. That factor alone counted greatly in his favour. There would be little awkward shuffling in order to reach him. But could he be relied upon?

Hayle decided that he would have to take the chance.

After another precautionary glance at the guard, Hayle rolled on to his back. This meant that his entire weight rested on his ankles and wrists. The pain was considerable, but it had to be endured. Very carefully, he wriggled towards the open food tin. When he was parallel with it, he rolled back on to his side, bringing his hands opposite the can. His wrists being lashed together meant that his fingers and palms were slightly apart. He groped until he contacted the can. He managed to get a moderately secure grip on it. Then he shuffled slowly and painfully towards Boroff.

The Russian was facing him. He was still rubbing his face on his shoulders. But suddenly he stopped doing this. He stared uncertainly at Hayle.

Hayle whispered: 'I think I can get you free. Understand?'

There was a pause. Then, reluctantly it seemed, Boroff gave a faint nod.

'I've got a food tin in my hands — the one with the open lid that Katz was holding. The edges are sharp. I want you to roll over so we're back to back. Then I'm going to try to cut your ropes. If I manage it, you must release me first. Then I'll see to the guard. But make no noise. Got it?'

Boroff's lips began trembling. Hayle thought: *He's going to bawl . . .*

But Boroff managed to control himself. He croaked: 'I don't want you to do that. I don't want to be cut free!'

'You don't? Why? Do you like the idea of being trussed up like a chicken?'

'It's impossible! We'd never manage it. The place is full of Arabs. We'd never get out.'

In his mounting exasperation, Hayle had to make an effort to keep his voice low.

'The Arabs are all sleeping. Once I've

fixed the guard, there's nothing to worry about.'

'But where would we go? We've no supplies now.'

'There are supplies in this tent. And these Arabs have mules and camels. We can use some of that transport. Don't you see — this is our chance!'

'Our chance? But why take a chance? The woman will show them where the coins are, then they'll go on their way and leave us alone!'

Hayle felt his leg muscles contract. They reflected an automatic desire to kick Boroff. 'Listen — I haven't had a chance of talking with Ruth, but she might have been bluffing! Maybe she was just trying to gain time!'

'I — I don't think she was bluffing. She didn't look as if she was.'

'Okay then, suppose she wasn't — do you trust the Arabs? I don't after what we did to them. They have a lot of reason for hating us. Now are you going to let me try to cut you loose?'

Another long pause. Boroff's lips were still quivering. Then he gave a sigh like the moan of an expiring animal and turned his back to Hayle.

Hayle got his back towards the Russian. In doing so, he dropped the can. It needed a full minute to retrieve it. Another couple of minutes went by while he adjusted his fingers and eased the can into position. Gradually his sense of touch developed and he was able to gauge tiny distances with some accuracy. He felt the jagged edge of the raised lid make contact with the ropes over Boroffs wrists.

It was an agonising operation, trying to saw through the bonds. His fingers throbbed with the effort of holding the can still. His wrists rebelled against the unnatural contortions. And progress was extremely slow because it was impossible to move the can more than an inch in either direction. Several times Hayle had to stop to rest. And after each rest there was further delay while he fumbled for the cutting area.

Once the Arab guard stirred suddenly, shook his head and opened his eyes. Hayle, who was facing him, had just enough warning to close his eyes and simulate sleep. He waited, tense. No movement came from the Arab. When Hayle peeped through slit lids, he saw the man was sleeping again.

He was still sleeping when, after nearly two hours' work, the ropes fell loose. Boroff did not move.

Hayle twisted round to face him. He hissed: 'You're okay now! Just pull your hands apart — there's nothing to stop them!'

Very slowly, Boroff obeyed. Hayle saw the ropes fall away. The Russian groaned. Hayle knew why. He was suffering cramp.

'Take your time,' Hayle said. 'Try to rub some life into your wrists.'

Boroff rubbed his wrists against his tunic. Then he flexed and unflexed his fingers. When the blood was flowing again, he did nothing save stare into space.

'Untie your legs! Don't sit around there admiring the scenery!'

Boroff bent forward. He picked with ghastly incompetence at the knots. At last, those too were free.

When Boroff tried to stand, he

promptly fell again. Cramp was in his legs, also. This gave Hayle a warning. He realised that even when the others were released, it would be several minutes before they were in a condition to move. And he himself would have to wait before attempting to deal with the Arab.

As he was assimilating this fact, Hayle glanced towards Ruth. She had not moved. Then at Katz. The German was looking directly at him. He must have been watching for some time. His slab of a face expressed excitement and hope.

Hayle whispered to Boroff: 'Don't worry about your legs yet. You don't need them. Just use your hands and set me free.'

Boroff remained sitting and staring into space, as if he had not heard the words.

'Do as I tell you. Untie these knots.'

Boroff answered. He did so with, for him, astonishing firmness. He said: 'I won't.'

'You won't? Don't be silly, Boroff!'

'I'm not crazy — really I'm not. I know we'd never get out of this camp. The Arabs would kill us. I think our best chance is to stay here and do as they say. If they find the coins, we'll be all right.'

'You fool! Do you like the idea of dying by inches?'

Boroff turned a contorted face towards Hayle. Tears were flowing again. It was then that Hayle realised the full extent of the man's moral collapse. Boroff always reacted to the wishes of the person of whom he was most afraid. He feared the Arabs more than any now. He did not fear Katz so much, for Katz was helpless.

Hayle made a last attempt. 'Listen, Boroff! If the Arabs find you as the only one who's free, they'll think you were the only one who wanted to escape. They'll blame you. They may kill you right away.'

Boroff shook his head. 'I don't think they will. Not if I explain to them what happened. I'm going to wake the guard and tell him.'

'Don't!'

'I must! I'll say it was all a mistake and I got free because I rubbed the ropes against a stone. They won't blame you.'

He walked unsteadily towards the Arab guard.

Dawn.

Masit said to them: 'If the legionnaire had not given himself up, I would not believe his story. But I am bound to do so.' He paused to survey them. Then he said: 'But your bonds have been cast aside now and you will help with the digging while the woman shows us where it is to be done.'

They began to move out of the tent, Ruth first, then Katz, Hayle following. Boroff brought up the rear.

Suddenly Katz stopped. He picked something from the ground. Holding it, he whirled round, pushing past Hayle. A scream of terror then a sob of pain went up from Boroff.

Katz muttered: 'Cowardly swine!'

And he dropped the open can on the ground. The jagged edge was stained with blood.

So was Boroff's face where it was ripped from an eyebrow to an ear.

10

Repulsed

They had the lush lustre of a dying sun. The fascination of a generous promise. They emerged out of the darkness of centuries to whisper of civilisations and peoples long gone.

They were nine Saracen coins. All were gold.

Masit caressed them in his crinkled hands. He rubbed them against his *burnous*. But he saw no beauty, no history in the unalloyed metal. Only cash value. Only purchasing power when he dealt with white traders on the banks of the Niger. And these nine coins were only the start. More would surely come . . .

The woman, he decided, had done well. There had been no deception. She had known precisely what she was about, when she directed the diggings in an almost untouched area. Masit looked at the men who were excavating the ditch below him. The three legionnaires were there, one of them with a badly injured face, and so were thirty of his men. The ten others he had posted as look-outs on the perimeters of the oasis. Masit wanted warning of any approach by other caravans.

Next, Masit let his gaze fall upon the woman. She was standing on the edge of the excavation ditch. There was an intensity about her. Occasionally she gave a brief direction or a suggestion. Mostly she was still, with her hands on her slim waist. She was a remarkable woman, Masit thought. A woman such as he, in his more virile days, would have been glad to possess. There was spirit within her. Courage, too.

Still fingering the coins, Masit regretfully turned his attention away from her. Subconsciously, he had been attracted by a movement on the northern perimeter. One of the *felaheen* he had posted there was running towards him and waving both hands above his head to stress the urgency of his mission.

When he arrived, the man had to pause for some moments before he collected sufficient breath to speak. When he did so, his words staggered Masit. 'Legionnaires are coming upon us!'

'Legionnaires! How many?'

The man shook his head and made a wild gesture which could have been indicative of any number. Masit cursed. He had a sense of loyalty towards his *felaheen*, but he knew that some of them panicked easily. This one, for example. It was stupidity to make such a report without first establishing the essential figures.

Still shaken, but rapidly collecting his wits, Masit strode forth to the northern edge of the oasis to see for himself.

The column was a long way off. It looked like a gently contorting snake on the shimmering horizon. But even at this distance, it was obvious that it was a very small column. He was glad to note that some of his men — more intelligent than the messenger — had moved out, so as to get a closer look. Masit, with growing confidence and a sense of hardening decision, patiently awaited their return.

They were back within five minutes. And their report confirmed Masit's view that he had little to fear.

'There are but two score of them,' one of them said, 'or perhaps a little more. And they are weary, Masit They walk like men condemned. I counted five of them who did not bear rifles.'

Masit was slightly incredulous. 'No rifles! Are you trying to please me with lies?'

The *felaheen* shook his head vigorously. 'On my oath, Masit, it is so.'

Masit's brow creased heavily in thought. Then he said: 'The legionnaires will receive a welcome from us. It will be just such a welcome as we received when we came to this place.'

★ ★ ★

Lieutenant Garnia was trying to rehearse a speech. But the trouble was that he could not get beyond the first sentence.

As soon as the oasis palms came in sight, he realised that he would have to

185

make some form of suitable explanation to the American archaeologists. He was going to ask them to sustain him and his men for a week or more. They would certainly want to know why it was they were in such a pitiable and unmilitary condition.

A terse explanation was required. One which would supply the essential truth without making him, as a French officer, appear ridiculous. But how did one explain to a group of scientists that one had lost a military post and all supplies, yet still retain a modicum of dignity? It was a baffling problem which, Garnia suspected, would even have defeated the great orators.

His opening phrase was clear enough. That was running through his head: *Messieurs, it is with profound regret that I have to tell you that* . . .

But tell them what? A French officer couldn't just announce that he was destitute because of a fire. He couldn't suavely explain that the men who were responsible for law and order in the area were now relying on a group of civilians for succour!

Garnia knew the American character. He knew their genius for dry ridicule. He winced at the prospect. He had no doubt that the archaeologists would receive them in a kindly fashion. *Mais Dieu!* But what would they think? What would they say to each other?

Garnia then realised anew that his embarrassments would not end at the oasis. *Non!* When in due course they were found, possibly by a spotter plane, he would have to face an enquiry. There might even be a court martial. In any case, it was clear to Garnia that his military career was drawing to a close. Excuses, however valid, were of no consequence. He had lost his post. He had lost millions of francs' worth of equipment and supplies. At the worst, he would be a figure of shame. At the best, one of mess-room levity.

He was surprised to realise that this prospect did not worry him too much. There was always Marie!

He longed for her. He had done so since he had first met her two years before at a military ball. But he had been compelled to endure the agony, for no officer without private resources could marry on a lieutenant's pay. But when he left the Legion, nothing could keep them apart. Certainly he would be able to get some sort of job — enough for them to live on. And they would be together always. No long separations such as a soldier must suffer.

Oui. He would live down his disgrace. And they would be happy, he and Marie . . .

He felt almost content. Except for that damnable feeling of tension. It came and went and came again like a turgid sea.

Yet there was nothing to worry about. Nothing at all. There was Lukka Oasis, scarcely two miles ahead. Looking very quiet, very peaceful. No sign of activity. But obviously, all would be resting from the afternoon heat. He would return immediately with mules to pick up the five legionnaires whom he had left in the desert. Then all he had to do was wait. How peaceful the oasis looked!

He could discern the outlines of the

tents. He thought now that he could make out just an occasional movement of men. But the heat haze made it impossible to be sure.

Garnia turned to Corporal Jurgan. '*Voila!* It is a welcome sight, is it not?'

Despite his exhaustion, Jurgan had resumed his normal state of beatific good humour. 'It is indeed, *mon officier*. It will be good to eat and drink well and then to rest. We are fortunate that it is an American expedition there, for they are hospitable people.

★　★　★

To Masit, it was clear that the legionnaires had come to the oasis to collect the deserters. And if that had been all they would have required, he might have accepted the situation peacefully.

But it was also obvious to him that when they found what had happened to the American expedition, they would remain at the oasis. And they would also put an abrupt stop to the search for further gold coins.

Masit's avaricious heart was determined to get all the gold possible from the ruins. A bedraggled column of legionnaires was not going to stop him. Here in Lukka was wealth. He would gain it. If legionnaires had to die, that was of little importance. The risk of the French being able to identify him later was negligible.

Carefully he deployed his men in defensive positions. Thirty of them were prone on the sand, facing the approaching column. Their rifles — mostly fairly efficient weapons — were loaded and sighted. The remaining ten were in the excavation ditch, out of sight, their knives pressing into the ribs of the three deserters and the woman.

Masit watched the column carefully from his position behind the cluster of palms. His latent warrior spirit emerged. This was going to be simple slaughter. An event worthy of the days of the Riff wars!

He prepared to give the signal for his *felaheen* to open fire.

★ ★ ★

Dieu! The oasis was less than half a mile off, and he still hadn't decided exactly what he would say to the archaeologists.

. . . it is with profound regret that I . . .

Why couldn't he receive verbal inspiration? Garnia slapped his hands together and gave it up. If the Americans wanted to snigger among themselves, then let them!

He looked back at his legionnaires. They were a sorry assembly. Weary beyond description, just as he was weary. One of them, in a worse condition even than the others, had dropped slightly behind. He was being helped by a comrade.

What was it that he had upbraided Jurgan for before they left the post? *Ah oui!* Jurgan had said it was a withdrawal. And he himself had insisted it was an advance. Advance south! Ludicrous . . .

Garnia turned his attention back to the oasis. He was slightly surprised that there was still no sign of activity. He had expected that by now people would be running towards them full of welcome and curiosity. But nothing stirred. He saw camels and mules tethered near the palms. He saw clearly the scarred markings which must be the excavations. But of human life — none. His nerve strings were whining.

All of a sudden, the skin of his face had drawn tight. He could hear the thundering of his own heart.

'*Arrete!*'

He gave the order to halt without fully realising that he was doing it. It was almost a reflex action. He had to repeat it twice before the column came to a shambling stop. It was entirely unexpected for the exhausted men.

Garnia turned to Jurgan. He was about to speak to him, but Jurgan interrupted. The corporal was pointing to the sand on the nearest edge of the oasis.

'*Mon officier!* Men are there! Watching us! I think — '

No one ever learned what it was that Corporal Jurgan thought. The Dutchman broke off the sentence abruptly and rolled his good-humoured eyes upwards until the whites showed. Then he lurched against Garnia before folding to the sand.

192

A bullet had entered the exact centre of his forehead and emerged through the top of his skull.

Garnia was scarcely aware of the end of his N.C.O. He was conscious only of a crash of rifle fire directly ahead of him. Of the whistle of slugs. And of a stupid tickling in his stomach.

What was it that lecturing staff officers called this sort of situation? *Ah oui!* They described it as a column of march under unexpected fire. That very phrase had been used by a bespectacled colonel in the junior conference room at Sidi Bel Abbes.

And what was the colonel's remedy? *Dieu!* What was it? An indolent Lieutenant Garnia had been dozing through that lecture, thinking of Marie. And now his stomach was tickling. And he felt a bit sick . . .

Take cover. Assess the situation. Appreciate the tactical problem before taking counter-action. That was what the colonel had said. It had sounded so damned easy. Hardly worth listening to.

Garnia staggered round to face his

column. *Sacre!* They did not need any orders! They must have heard about the colonel's lecture. They had taken cover of their own accord. All of them were flat on the sand. And he was the only one still standing.

He threw himself down as the second volley passed over his head. His brain was beginning to work properly again. The moments of fuddled hysteria had gone.

He looked at Jurgan. Jurgan was dead. He did not look at all good-humoured now. Just vaguely repulsive with that mess coming out of his head. And a fly was already buzzing over it. Damn all flies!

Garnia waved a cautious hand at the men behind him. 'Spread out!' he shouted.

At first they did not move. They looked at him blankly, when they looked at all, temporarily stunned by events.

'For God's sake, spread out! You'll all be killed if you're huddled here!'

This time they obeyed. Their background of rigid training was asserting itself. Pushing their Lebels ahead of them, they dragged themselves along with their elbows. Bullets began to spray sand among them as they formed a widely spaced line facing the oasis.

But not all of them moved. Some of them remained still or nearly still. Garnia made a quick examination, crawling among them.

Seven men were dead. Two were dying and nothing could be done for them.

Deliberately, he listened for the next volley. He also risked raising his head slightly to study the position whence it came. It immediately became obvious to him that they were outnumbered by at least two to one.

And what had happened at the oasis? If only he knew. He was like a blind man trying to grapple with an enemy who could see.

But for the moment they were relatively safe. Already the rifle fire was becoming less intense. The enemy — whoever the enemy were — had realised that while the legionnaires remained prone, it was almost impossible to hit them.

That tickling in Garnia's belly had become more intense. It was almost a pain now. He looked.

Dieu! His tunic was stained a moist reddish purple. That was blood. His own blood. And the stuff was wasting onto the sand.

He found a soiled handkerchief and folded it into a tight pad. Then he pressed it against the wound and he tried to forget it. He was attempting to make an appreciation of the tactical problem.

★   ★   ★

Masit was almost satisfied.

He wished that all the legionnaires had been destroyed by the first volley, but he could not blame his *felaheen* for the fact that they were not. He had intended to wait until the column was much closer before giving the order to open fire. It was that sudden halt of the legionnaires, obviously caused by suspicion, which had compelled him to act earlier than he had intended.

But it was clear that the few who remained out there were no menace. They might stay flat on the sand until nightfall and then withdraw. If they did, they could retreat without hindrance. But if they showed themselves while daylight remained, they would be mown down.

Meantime, Masit decided that the digging for coins could be resumed. He knew that he could not spare any of his own men for the task. But the three legionnaires could still do it, under the guidance of the woman and the supervision of the guards.

After a final survey of the scene of static conflict, Masit left the palms. He moved to the excavation site and smiled as he looked down into the deep ditch.

The four captives were being held against the opposite parapet. Their faces reflected an intermingling of wonder, fear and anger. The *felaheen* still had knives pressed firmly against their ribs.

The flow of events was adding greatly to Masit's confidence. That he was a shrewd man of commerce he had always known. But now he suspected that he also had latent genius as a warrior.

He said with smooth composure: 'That

was a Legion column which tried to visit us just now.'

Hayle regarded him steadily, but his voice was toneless as he said: 'We know that. Our guards told us. What's happened to them, Masit?'

Masit made a broad and generous gesture. 'Many are dead. The others lie flat to the ground, unable to move without being slain. They are helpless, for we greatly outnumber them. But don't look so angry, legionnaire! Surely you do not want to fall into their hands!'

He waited for a reaction to the taunt. There was none, so he said: 'And now you will continue with your digging.'

★   ★   ★

Towards sunset, they unearthed the major cache of coins. It was Katz who first revealed the hiding place. His spade probed round what at first seemed to be a fragment of tesselated paving, but it was soon shown to be a flap over a small square hole. Within that hole, amid the dust of the leather bags which had once

198

contained them, were many hundreds of gold and silver pieces.

The Arabs looked at them with awe. Then they talked among themselves in excitement. It was obvious to the most untutored eye that here was wealth in unsuspected abundance.

Masit was fetched. His frame twitched with pleasure. He gloated long over the hoard without attempting to touch it. Then he ordered a transfer of the coins to a goatskin sack. He counted them aloud during this process. It took a considerable amount of time. In all, there were nearly six hundred of them.

Two Arabs moved the treasure to a tent. Masit watched it go as one seeing the temporary departure of a dear friend. Then he spoke to Ruth, who was still in the ditch.

'You have done well, woman. Your tongue did not lie.'

She brushed fair hair away from her dusty face. 'I've kept my word. Are you going to keep yours?'

'I am, for I'm a man of honour. Soon it will be night. Then we will withdraw, leaving the oasis to you.'

Hayle said: 'The legionnaires — they'll go after you.'

'I don't think so. There are too few of them and they are too weary. In any case, we have camels. They could not pursue us. Rather do I think that they, too, will withdraw during the night, and for that you will be grateful — for you would not wish them to move in here to seize you?'

Katz looked hopeful. He said almost ingratiatingly: 'Then we will be no worse off than before you came! We can remain here in the oasis, waiting for a caravan!'

Masit turned his palms upwards and inclined his head. It was a faintly cynical movement.

'Not so! Of course you can wait here if you wish, but you will soon cry out for water!'

'Water!' Hayle said sharply. 'There's plenty of it in the well.'

'Even so. And it will remain in the well. But you will not be able to drink it. Not for many months. For I can do without one of my mules.'

Hayle looked at him in bafflement.

'What have your mules got to do with it, Masit?'

'I will have one of them slain — it is a little lame, anyway. Its corpse will be split open. Then it will be dropped into the water.'

They needed time to absorb this information. Time to appreciate the implications of it.

Hayle was the first to recover. He rasped: 'You can't know what you're doing! To poison the well would be more than a crime against us. It would be a crime against all your own people who use this caravan route!'

'A caravan would always carry sufficient water to reach the next oasis.'

'But why do this to us? You promised we could go free.'

'I *am* letting you go free.'

'Free to die of thirst!'

'That is not so. You could, if you wished, go over to the Legion column. Even if they withdraw before we do, you would still be able to overtake them. They would give you water, perhaps.'

Katz spoke in tones near to a snarl. He

said: 'They might keep us alive for a little time. But they would kill us later!'

Masit shrugged. 'That is not my concern. But I will tell you — I have a more important reason for poisoning the water than vengeance against you. I know that if fresh soldiers pursue us, they will have to come this way. If they find no fresh water here, they will have to turn back.'

Katz and Hayle realised the truth of this. There was a possibility, though a slim one, that a troop of *tirailleurs*, the mounted Sengalese, might be warned in time. They used horses. If the Lukka Oasis were useless, they would have to give up the chase. Their position was quite different from that of a caravan using camels. The *tirailleurs'* mounts needed frequent watering.

But Boroff did not realise the truth of it. He was not even listening, but fingering his mauled face, rubbing the crusts of dried blood on it and staring in a peculiar fashion at Katz. He knew that it was a cruel wound he bore. One which would certainly mark him for life

— however long or short that may be. Allowed to run its course, it would settle into a repulsive scar.

Boroff had been secretly proud of his appearance. He considered that his thin and weak face was suggestive of fine breeding. In an existence of fear and misery, an occasional glimpse of his own face was one of his few consolations. Drink was another.

And now he was a creature of horror! A man from whom other men would turn away! And women? The cruel might smile. The kind (the worst of all) might pretend not to notice.

He played with the wound. He continued to watch Katz. Suddenly Boroff's heart bounded. He had just made an astounding discovery.

He no longer feared Katz! God! He no longer feared anyone!

The open food can had done it! As it ripped across his flesh, it had cured him.

In that Satanic moment, he had reached the ultimate of terror. The glimpse of the fiendish face, the instantaneous knowledge of what was about to happen, the hot pain of the jagged edge . . .

No man could have known greater fear. He could never know its like again. For now all fear was gone. It had burned itself out. Expired in one last sear of flame.

But it had not left a vacuum. No. There was something just as strong in its place: hate. Hate for Legionnaire Katz. For everything he stood for. The domination of the strong over the weak. The superiority of physical power over mental power. If the beliefs of men like Katz were right, then the dominant animal on earth ought to be the elephant. Not humanity.

Boroff was leaning on his spade. He was standing slightly behind the others in the ditch. And his fevered brain noted for the first time that Masit, Hayle, and occasionally Katz were talking avidly. Whatever they were saying must be very important, because even the Arab guards had relaxed their vigilance to listen. But he was not interested in their mere words. It was action that Boroff wanted. Action to kill Katz.

It would be easy. The German was only

a couple of feet off. And his massive back was half turned to him.

Tingling with excitement, Boroff raised the spade. No one had noticed. He balanced himself.

He swung it at Katz's head. Swung it viciously.

There was sand adhering to it. It was the sand which warned Katz. Particles of it preceded the swing of the spade. They hit his face. Automatically he darted back. That brought him within the arc of the improvised weapon. Instead of being struck by steel, the wood shaft made a comparatively weak contact with his cheek.

Katz was knocked slightly off balance. But only slightly. And he could think very fast. As he reeled, he twisted his big body and projected himself at Boroff. He wrenched the spade out of Boroff's hands. Boroff jumped back a couple of paces. Then he leapt for the parapet and tried to climb up it.

It chanced that he was directly under the spot where Masit was standing. He saw Masit's legs. It was a natural reaction to grab for those legs so as to help the climb. And it was also natural that Masit lost his balance.

The bewildered Arab toppled towards the ditch. At the same moment, Katz was swinging the spade at Boroff. Masit's descending body got in the way of the swing. The sharp edge of the spade sliced completely through the Arab's scrawny neck. His head rolled among the excavations, yards away from his still twitching body.

Stillness.

For long seconds, an utterly complete absence of movement.

Katz still retained the spade, looking stupidly at the blooded steel. Boroff remained half up the parapet, one leg swung over the top.

Hayle and Ruth stood together a few yards away. She was leaning back against his chest.

The guards stared, transfixed, at the decapitated body.

It was one of the guards who broke the evil magic. He was naturally an excitable man. And one who, like the others, was much attached to Masit. He gave a nerve-shaking wail. He dropped his knife and drummed his fists against his breast. Then, without further warning, he scrambled out of the ditch and ran towards the oasis perimeter to where the others were crouched, their rifles trained on the legionnaires.

He screamed. In his dialect he screamed that Masit was gone. That they were leaderless. That they were lost.

It was an unduly pessimistic view. But hysteria is a disease. It is infectious, particularly in moments of exceptional shock. It spread first to the other guards in the ditch. Some joined the wailing. The others knelt at the side of the ghastly remains. For the time, they had forgotten about the three legionnaires and the woman. No desire for vengeance. In the normal course of human emotion, that would come later. It needed time — just a little time — to develop.

But the greatest impact was on the Arabs on the perimeter. At first, they were confused at the spectacle of one of their fellows rushing towards them from the rear, screaming. As they understood his words, confusion blossomed into panic. They gathered only one fact clearly. That Masit was dead. By what strange nightmare this had happened, they could not fully comprehend.

And they wanted to know.

Singly at first, then in groups, they emerged from their places of cover and converged upon the messenger.

★   ★   ★

Garnia watched in wonderment. But not for long. In a hoarse voice he called an order. '*Baionettes!*'

His handful of legionnaires rose to one knee. They fumbled with scabbards. There was a faint hiss as the lengths of steel were simultaneously extracted. A harsher click as they were clipped under the Lebel barrels.

'*En avant, mes braves!*'

They got to their feet. A tattered, gaunt, weary group. They stumbled rather than charged towards the oasis.

Somehow Garnia kept in the lead, even

though his stomach felt as if a white hot piece of coal had been inserted in it. Even though he knew a ghastly sensation of weakness.

A wild, almost delirious thought was circulating through his head. *It's an advance after all!* he told himself. *It's an advance south . . .*

★   ★   ★

The Arabs recovered in time — but only partially.

There was no fight in them, though if they had turned to do so, they would surely have decimated the legionnaires.

They did no more than run for their camels and mules and drive them half loaded, half harnessed, out into the darkening desert.

★   ★   ★

Garnia slumped into a chair in the main tent. It was cold now with the arrival of night. But his body felt like a furnace. Sweat was thick on his brow. Under his tunic he pressed the sopping pad against his wound.

It had been a tremendous effort, concentrating on what the three deserters had to say. Almost impossible at times to make sense of it all. But now at last he knew in outline what had happened. He would speak to the woman later.

He coughed. It was intended to be a brief cough, but it continued for a long time. Blood was welling into his throat.

When he managed to speak, he knew that his voice sounded unreal, like the utterances of a broken robot.

'You are under close arrest,' he said. 'You insult the uniform you wear . . . all three of you. In due time you will face a court martial. I hope and believe you will be shot.'

11

The Skies

The colonel was emphatic. 'This,' he told his bored adjutant, 'is base headquarters. Is it not?'

The adjutant agreed that it was.

'And being such, we ought to be in touch with every fort and every post in the command area. Instantaneous touch. But I resolve to make an urgent communication to Post D and what happens? Go on — tell me! What happens?'

'Er — nothing happened.'

'That is so. Our radio signal is repeated at half-hourly intervals for this entire day. And silence is our only answer. *Sacre!* It is bad!'

'It's not unusual,' the adjutant suggested. 'Radio transmitters often develop trouble in these posts. The heat harms the batteries. And all of them are old sets.'

'It is no use making excuses. You know the urgency of the message!'

'*Ah oui.* You want to make sure that Lieutenant Garnia visits Lukka Oasis in person.'

'Exactly. Until today I had not fully realised the significance of this American archaeological expedition. I cannot think of everything — I have much to do. But the fact remains that the Americans are important people. It is not enough that they should be given permits to enter our territory and then be merely visited by a patrol under an N.C.O. And that is precisely what I fear Garnia will do. He will not want to visit the place himself. But I insist that Garnia, as a French officer, personally makes a courtesy call on our . . . our distinguished guests. But now I cannot communicate with him by radio. What do I have to do?'

The adjutant, who had been trotting between the radio room and colonel's office for most of the day, was reaching the limit of his patience. 'You will have to trust to Lieutenant Garnia's common sense.'

'I will not! No one should ever trust a subaltern's common sense. It would be like leaning on an invisible support. It's hardly ever there. *Non!* I will have to send an aircraft out to the post. An aircraft! Think of the expense. I will have to account for that in due course!'

The adjutant looked thoughtful. There was scarcely concealed malice in his words. 'Would it not be best, *mon colonel*, if you yourself travelled in the plane? You could go straight on to Lukka and make a personal courtesy call. Your rank! Your status! It would be most impressive.'

'*Mais non!* I would like to do that, of course! But you know my responsibilities here. They would not permit! No! The plane will go as far as the post and no further. The lieutenant can do his own donkey work. He will benefit from some exercise, no doubt. I will make out a written order telling him to visit the oasis.'

'We will also need a written requisition for the use of a small transport plane.'

'I will sign that, too.'

Marie was very near him. He could feel the touch of her hands, stroking back his damp hair. Cool yet firm. She was talking to him . . .

But that wasn't Marie's voice! The words which came distantly to his ears were not spoken with the French inflections Marie used. Here was the different accent of a foreigner. An American.

Suddenly his eyes were open. The world was clear again. Too clear. In his stomach there was foul agony.

The American woman was bending over him, speaking softly. What was her name? For the moment, he could not remember.

She was saying: 'Don't try to sit up, lieutenant. Don't try . . . '

He was on a camp bed in the main tent. 'What happened to me, *m'selle*? I don't remember anything except talking to the deserters.'

'You collapsed. I've looked at your wound.'

He realised the soiled and sopping handkerchief had been taken away. Now there was a bandage of clean linen across his stomach.

'You . . . you did this for me?'

'I did. But it's not enough. There's a bullet in there, I think . . . deep in. It's got to be taken out. Only a doctor can do it.'

But he was not listening. Recollections flooded back. He thought of a place in the desert. 'I cannot think about myself, *m'selle*. There are others . . . their condition may be worse than mine.'

She smiled gently and pressed a water-soaked pad against his brow. 'I don't think they can be in a worse fix than you, Lieutenant Garnia. You need — '

'There are five men out there in the desert. They cannot walk. They have little food and water. I promised to reach them by evening. What's the time?'

'Almost dawn.'

'*Dieu!* They'll think I've forgotten them — or sacrificed them. I would have returned immediately, but the men here are weary and there are no camels or mules for transport. But we'll leave soon after daylight. They ought to survive another day.'

Ruth said firmly: '*You* won't leave, lieutenant.'

'*Oui!* I must. I — '

'You can't. You know you can't. You must send others.'

An exceptionally fierce spasm of pain proved to him the truth of her words. He almost cried out. When it had passed, he looked at her.

'I remember . . . your name's Westlake — Ruth Westlake.'

He had to break off because blood had surged back into his throat. When he had finished coughing, he added: 'I was going to ask for a report from you. I have the duty of — '

'You'll get your report when you feel better. I think you'll have been told most about me.'

He nodded feebly, then added: 'M'selle . . . *you* may laugh at this, but a few moments ago, just before I awoke, I thought you were Marie. I thought it was Marie who was touching me.'

216

'Marie? Is she — '

'We were to have been married as soon as I became a captain.'

'Were to! You're going to! But first you've got to get that bullet out.'

This time his smile was genuine. But it was a sad smile. '*Merci, m'selle*, but I think not. Yet — I would have liked to have seen Marie just once again.'

Involuntarily, she kneeled beside him, saying: 'You must love her very much.'

'*Oui, m'selle*.'

'Does she like your being a soldier? I suppose she's proud of you. French women are always very proud of their men in uniform.'

'Marie doesn't like me being a soldier. I think I haven't liked it very much, for it has kept us apart.'

He broke off, staring at her hair through dull eyes. But there was a touch of Gallic gallantry about him as he added: 'But you, you are very beautiful, *m'selle*. Have you ever been in love?'

She did not answer. Instead, she again bathed his brow. But he persisted.

'Tell me — have you?'

217

It was a challenge. She took it. 'I *am* in love, lieutenant. But it's hopeless. The man will probably die very soon.'

'As I am going to die?'

'Don't be stupid! You'll be fine.'

'Is he an American, like you?'

She nodded. 'And like you, lieutenant, he's a soldier. In some ways, you two are very alike — kind and brave and very loyal.'

'To me, you're too kind. I suppose he's in the American Army?'

'He was in the United States Air Corps.'

'And now?'

'Now, Lieutenant Garnia, he's in the French Foreign Legion.'

He turned his head from her, staring up at the apex of the tent. He whispered: 'Is it one of the deserters? Legionnaire Hayle?'

For a brief moment she lost her self-control. She sobbed. It was a clear enough answer.

'Tell me about him,' he said. 'I have heard a story from all three deserters, but the American alone would not say much.

Tell me everything.'

She told him. At first the words came slowly. Then they gathered momentum. When she finished, she was sobbing again.

And for a long time, Garnia was silent. Then he murmured: 'It is strange . . . strange that I should be losing my woman . . . and you your man . . . '

He broke off to clutch the bandage over his stomach. He gasped under the torment.

When he had recovered a little, he added: 'I wish with all my heart I could help you, *m'selle*, for I believe all you say of the legionnaire. And I knew about his mother. But even his colonel could do nothing for him. And I can do even less, now that he is guilty of desertion. He will remain under arrest, and he will face a court martial when we are relieved. Please, *m'selle* — you have not known him for long. Try to forget him. It would for the best.'

★   ★   ★

Captain Toulez was peeved as he guided his light transport plane at a low altitude over the Algerian Desert. He considered that if there was any justice left on earth, it had given him a very decisive miss. That morning he had been hoping to take his plane west to St. Louis on the Senegal coast to pick up recently landed medical supplies. That would have entailed at least a whole day in the town. There was good wine at St. Louis.

But during the night he had been given orders to depart before dawn for a new destination. For a confounded Legion post. And there he was to deliver a letter containing some balderdash written by the colonel. It was too exasperating. Too unjust.

Captain Toulez spoke to himself. Since there was no one else to speak to, it was a fair substitute.

'The colonel did not stop to think of the strain an air pilot lives under,' he said darkly. 'We need rest.'

He muttered on for a while. Then it occurred to him to check his position. Switching on the automatic pilot control, he got busy. With no landmarks, it was impossible to get an exact fix. But he was confident that after two hours' flying at a steady air speed of one hundred and fifty miles an hour, he was somewhere approaching Post D.

Captain Toulez decided to gain height so as to have a wider view of the rolling red wastes. It was five minutes later, from an altitude of three thousand feet, that he saw the walls of Post D a few degrees to the south-west. He consoled his mood with a little self-congratulation.

'I am a magnificent airman,' he said. 'My navigation, it is impeccable! *Sacre!* But I am worthy of better treatment. I ought — '

There was no roof to the building in the post! Only a few charred timbers. He could see them quite clearly. And there was no sign of life in the place.

Captain Toulez pushed forward the control column until he was down to five hundred feet. At that level he flattened out, then eased his two throttles to only a little above stalling speed. The plane almost ambled over the post.

'*Dieu!* It is all burned!'

As he was making the run, Toulez

caught a glimpse of some large stones in the compound. They were laid out in the form of writing. But he was not able to read them.

Three miles beyond the post, he turned. He gained height again. This time he could read the message clearly.

'*Fire. All stores lost. Garrison evacuated to Lukka.*'

Captain Toulez forgot his sense of injustice. He forgot everything save a desire to communicate with base air control. With sweating fingers, he dragged on his headphones and mouthpiece. He spoke rapidly and urgently to an astonished controller sitting in a stifling stone box at the military airport three hundred miles away.

Then Toulez cruised up and down over the post, awaiting orders. It was another fifteen minutes before they came.

'*You are to proceed to Lukka. Make a report from there. Inform Lieutenant Garnia that a troop plane with men and supplies will arrive before sunset.*'

Toulez checked his map reference. Then he turned his plane until the compass indicated due south.

It seemed only moments afterwards that he spotted an unnatural smudge on the sand. A blot of uncertain colour, save for moving blobs of pink.

He made a careful landing on the uneven surface. And as the five legion-naires hobbled frantically towards his plane, Toulez said: 'I think this is more interesting than a day in St. Louis. *Dieu!* I wonder what will happen to me next.'

He arrived at Lukka just in time to stop ten legionnaires from setting out to bring back the five.

12

Encounter

To permit ventilation, the flap of the prison tent was slightly open. Katz glared through it and glared over the shoulders of the legionnaire on guard outside, then towards the small transport plane which stood two hundred yards away, tail towards them.

Katz had been standing like that for a long time, hands on his barrel-like waist, bristled jowls twitching. Suddenly he wheeled round. He faced Hayle and Boroff. Hayle was stretched on the ground, eyes open but blank, face expressionless. Boroff was sitting on his haunches, drawing aimless designs with his fingers in the sand. In his face there was hate. It intensified as he looked up at Katz.

Katz said: 'Listen to me! I have something to say!'

Neither of his audience moved. Neither spoke.

Katz advanced into the centre of the tent so that he glowered between the two. Then he lowered his voice as he said: 'You heard what the sentry told us — troops are being flown out here. They'll arrive before sunset. It's past midday now.'

Hayle did not look at Katz as he said: 'We heard. Is that all you've got to tell us?'

'*Nein*. Now hear me. We can still get away. There is still a chance.'

'I think I can guess what's in your mind,' Hayle said tonelessly. 'But carry on. I'm listening.'

'You know, my friends, what will happen to us when the troop plane arrives? Soon it will fly back — and we will be inside it. Then we are finished — *phut*!'

He accompanied the exclamation by spitting in the approximate direction of Boroff. The Russian did not move. He continued to gaze malevolently at Katz.

Katz continued, still keeping his voice

225

down: 'That aircraft — if we could seize it . . . '

Hayle interrupted: 'I thought that was your master plan, Katz. It's the kind of idea you just couldn't miss. Maybe you haven't noticed, but there's still a sentry outside this tent. And there are quite a few legionnaires close by. We'd get a bullet each in of our guts before we got halfway.'

Katz rubbed his rough chin. He grimaced. It was suggestion of superior knowledge. 'That is where you are wrong, my friend. I have looked through the flap. I have looked also under these tent walls. And what have I seen? I have seen the one armed man outside here and four armed men posted on the borders of the oasis. The others are sleeping. They are still worn from their march.'

'That's still five armed men, Katz. They could do a lot of shooting.'

'*Nein!* Don't you see — the four on the borders are too far away! We could be in the aircraft before they knew what was happening. In the air, even!'

'And the sentry outside this tent?'

226

'I can manage him, my friend . . . ' Katz extended his big hands. 'From behind I can snatch his neck. With my knee I can press into his spine. His back will break in but a moment — like an old twig! He will not have time even to cry out!'

They were silent for a time. Then Hayle said: 'Go ahead, Katz.'

'Ah, good! You agree! Then let us prepare.'

'You prepare. I'm not.'

'You're not . . . ? But you must. We need you. You were an airman. You alone can fly the machine.'

Slowly, Hayle sat up. He stretched and yawned. There was still no expression in his face. Only an indifferent lethargy.

He said: 'Get this straight, Katz. I've had enough. I've tried to quit without doing anyone any harm. It hasn't worked out that way. I'm not going to make it any worse than it is. I wanted to see my home as much as either of you. I still do. But I know now that the cards have fallen for me. We were doomed and blasted before we started. That's the way it is and, I'm not squealing. I've lost and I'll take my beating.'

Katz regarded him with a complete lack of comprehension. It was an ethical statement which confounded his own limited sense of morality.

'My friend — you mean you want to surrender? You want to die?'

'No, Katz, I don't want either of those things. But I can't see any way of avoiding them — and your plan isn't the sort of get-out I can take to.'

There was a fatalistic finality about his words. Slowly it dawned on Katz that he had to accept them. He cursed. But soon he became tired of that. He went back to the tent flap and peered out. He was there for only a few moments. When he turned again, his face bore a flush of excitement. He looked down at Boroff. And Boroff looked steadily back, fingering his unsightly face.

Katz said hoarsely: 'Do you wish to escape, my little fool?'

Without shifting his eyes, Boroff nodded. 'I might, Katz.'

'Then listen — we must act fast! The

air captain — he's now standing beside the plane. There is our pilot! I will handle the sentry and take his Lebel. We will not hesitate! Not for a moment! We will rush for the plane. At rifle point, we will force the pilot to take the air with us aboard, and for Spanish territory! You understand? If we are strong, it will be easy!'

Boroff said slowly: 'Why do you want to take me? Once you wanted to kill me, remember? And yesterday I tried to kill you.'

Deliberately, Katz's face assumed a semblance of a smile. 'I want to take you because you will be a great help, Boroff. You are not a man. *Nien!* You are a poor rabbit. You could not even kill me when my back turned! But the pilot will not know what a weakling you are! Two of us will frighten him more than one. Now quick — are you ready?'

Boroff rose from his haunches. 'I'm ready, Katz,' he said.

Hayle was also on his feet. The lethargy had left him. He moved towards Katz. He said: 'Get this, Katz — you're not going to murder that sentry. He's a — '

Katz kicked viciously. His boot landed against the lower part of Hayle's stomach. Hayle's jaw fell open. He swayed, then slumped on to his face, unconscious.

Katz turned towards the tent flap. The sentry's back was less than a foot outside. Katz extended his massive arms. His thick fingers dug towards the man's trachea. He pulled backwards. And at the same time he pressed his left knee into the centre of the legionnaire's spine.

The man remained bent backwards for a moment like a contortionist. Then he relaxed. The relaxation was accompanied by a faint snapping sound as a vertebra dislocated. He was dead as Katz dragged him into the tent and whipped the rifle out of his slack hands.

Katz gave Boroff a powerful push which projected him out of the tent. Together they ran towards the plane, where Captain Toulez was making an inspection of the undercarriage.

Toulez was not aware of their approach until they were almost on him, for the running feet made little sound on the sand. He saw Katz first. He had a bewildered impression of an enormous man aiming a rifle at him. Then an even less clear picture of a tiny legionnaire in the rear.

Katz came to a slithering, panting stop. He pushed the rifle muzzle deep into Toulez's stomach. Toulez tried to back away.

'Stay where you are!'

For a moment it occurred to Toulez that the legionnaires might be stricken with sun madness. He had heard of such a thing happening. Then he remembered the deserters. His bones turned soft. His brain became a terrified whirlpool. This was the first time in his service career that Captain Toulez had been in physical danger. He was making the unpleasant discovery that he was a coward.

'What — is it you want?'

'Are you ready to die — slowly?'

'*Oh, non!*'

'Then, my friend, get into that plane and take off immediately. Fly west.'

'I — I can't do that . . . I have no authority . . .'

'Here's your authority — this Lebel.

Are you ready to challenge it?'

'*Non*, but — '

'Get into the plane! We will be behind you. *Now!*'

Captain Toulez whimpered. He looked frantically around. Far off, he could see a Legion sentry on the perimeter running towards them. He seemed to be shouting. But he was too distant to be of any assistance.

The wretched airman turned towards the side door the plane. He extended a shaking, palsied hand and opened it. There he hesitated again, but only because his quivering muscles rebelled at the effort of climbing inside.

Katz lowered his rifle. He extended his left hand, intending to help the pilot. But Katz was not watching Boroff.

Boroff was picking up a small piece of rock — a very sharp rock, with a multitude of edges. He weighed it thoughtfully. And with a full swing of his arm, he brought it down onto the top of Katz's head.

Katz's kepi offered no more protection than a sheet paper. A small area of the

232

skull collapsed inwards like tapped eggshell. The man was already dead as fell forward against Toulez. The impact knocked him off the step which he had just mounted. He dropped back to the ground. It seem as if he was going to fall on top of Katz. But recovered balance in time to see Boroff seizing the rifle which lay under the German.

Boroff might have succeeded in the second phase of his plan if he had been more patient, and not given Toulez premature warning. He was still digging the weapon free when he screamed over his shoulder: 'Get into the plane! Things are just the same for you! You're still flying out of here — but you're to have only one passenger. Do you see? Only me!'

Toulez, who had been semi-paralysed by the German, found that the puny little Russian had no such effect upon him. Particularly since the Russian was not yet even in a position to shoot at him.

But even then, Toulez hesitated. He assessed the risk before darting a hand at his revolver holster.

There would have been no risk if he

had acted immediately. As it was, he extracted his revolver at the same moment that Boroff straightened up with his rifle. He pulled on the trigger, stiff with lack of use and oil, in the same second that Boroff took aim at him.

There was a fine point of distinction about the double execution. Toulez intended to kill Boroff. In a vague manner, he had visions of receiving military honours for his intrepid resistance to two deserters. But Boroff did not intend to slay Toulez. Boroff needed Toulez. All he wanted to do was to frighten the man into submission. The Russian was overlooking the fact that he had never at any time frightened anyone.

The bullet which entered Boroff's chest caused a reflex action of his trigger finger. The Lebel, held at waist level, gave a solidly crashing report.

The two men fell on top of Katz.

★   ★   ★

Garnia saw it all. Saw it very clearly from his camp bed. So did Ruth, standing taut just within the tent entrance.

As the two almost simultaneous shots died away, Garnia began to cough again. She went to him and helped him. When the spasm had passed, he said faintly: 'Your American legionnaire . . . he was not there.'

She shook her head.

Garnia added: 'Look at the prison tent, *s'il vous plait.*'

Slowly, she went outside. Her mind was numb again under the lash of horror. She was glad he had not attempted that escape. Yet, yet . . .

Oh God! Yes . . . what had they done to him . . . ?

She was frightened. She went back to Garnia and said: 'They may have . . . can I go to the tent? I want to be the first . . . '

Garnia managed to nod. Ruth was about to leave when he stopped her. He said: 'If he is dead? If they have killed him because he did not want to join them, what then, *m'selle?*'

She half turned towards him. 'Look at me, lieutenant! Look at my face. Remember, if you can, everything that I've told you. And remember that I'm a woman. Will you let that be your answer?'

'It's a good answer, *m'selle*. If it is possible, bring him to me.'

★   ★   ★

Hayle was getting to his feet as she came in. He did not see her. And she did not want him to see her. Not yet. She wanted only to stand there within the threshold, watching and giving silent thanks.

He staggered towards the centre pole and leaned against it, his head resting against an arm, eyes concealed. His broad shoulders were shaking.

At first she did not realise that he was weeping. No tears, perhaps. But weeping just the same.

Ruth did not move as she said softly: 'Eddie . . . '

He jerked his arm away and spun round to face her. It was as she had thought: his eyes were dry. But his mouth was turned down at the corners and the lips were slack.

But his voice was the negation of his

appearance. It was harsh, rough. He said: 'What are you doing here? Are you gloating over me because I've had enough?'

'Do I look as if I'm gloating, Eddie? I came because . . . because of what's happened.'

'I saw what happened — I expected it.'

'Didn't they want to take you?'

'They wanted to, but I didn't. Katz put me out.'

Ruth moved towards him until she was standing very close. Then she asked: 'The plan might have worked if you'd been with them, Eddie. Don't you still want to get home?'

He answered savagely: 'Don't talk about it! I don't want to think about it! I don't want to think about anything! I'm a guy without a future. I've only got a present and a past.'

She persisted gently: 'Eddie, why didn't you go with them?'

He looked at her steadily. When he spoke, his voice was intense. But the ferocity had gone. 'Ruth . . . I didn't go because I can't. I wanted to get out of this outfit — but I wanted to do it the right way. Okay, the Legion couldn't let me do it right, so I decided to quit. But I didn't count on having to kill guys who are just like myself. I'm not a killer — not like Katz was. I've . . . I've taken enough. Now I'll face what's coming to me and I'll try not to squawk.'

She raised her hands until they touched his cheeks. She pulled his head down and whispered: 'I never did like guys who squawked, Eddie.'

It was several minutes before he freed her from his embrace. And their arms were round each other as they walked towards Garnia's tent.

★   ★   ★

Garnia was coughing again when they went in. Hayle stood awkwardly beside the camp bed while Ruth attended to him. His face seemed suddenly to have lost its last semblance of tan. It was a pale grey, and there were pouches of vivid purple under his eyes.

When his throat was temporarily clear,

he looked wearily up at Hayle. 'There's . . . there's no need to seem so sympathetic, legionnaire,' he said. 'There is no pain now. It's quite gone.'

Hayle said uncertainly: 'I'm glad, *mon officier*. You'll be okay.'

Garnia shook his head. '*Non*. It is not a sign of recovery . . . it's a sign of death, *mon ami*.'

Hayle sought for words of contradiction. But Garnia silenced him with a feeble flutter of a hand. 'My tunic . . . it's at the bottom of my bed, legionnaire. Would you . . . '

Hayle passed it to him. Slowly, Garnia opened a breast pocket. He extracted a leather case and opened it. A tinted photograph of a dark-haired woman was revealed. He studied it for some seconds. Then he said simply: 'That is Marie — my Marie.'

He held the picture out. Ruth took it. She said: 'Marie's very lovely. You're lucky, lieutenant.'

'Lucky to have known her — *oui*. But she will never be mine. I will lose her. Such stupidity! But . . . but would it not be a twice greater stupidity if you should lose him when there is no need for you to do so?'

They regarded him blankly.

Garnia struggled to a semi-upright position. His voice became stronger. 'You were an air pilot, lieutenant?'

'Yes, but — '

'There is a plane out there. It needs a pilot. Take it — both of you.'

Hayle did not move for a moment. Then he shook his head. 'I can't, *mon officier.*'

'Can't? And why?'

'For one thing, I'm not quitting anymore. For another, you'd be held responsible.'

Garnia's lips did not turn. But there was a hint of a smile in his dying eyes as he said: 'No man can hold me responsible for what I do now, lieutenant. You know that. And you talk of not running away anymore, but you will not be running away. You will be obeying an order. I order you to take that plane. I order you to take the lady. And to fly into the territory of Spain.'

He was weak with the force of his words. Hayle remained still.

'It's an easy way out, lieutenant, but I can't — '

'You can! You must! There is little time . . . soon the troop plane will be here, then nothing can be done. Remember — I am still your officer, legionnaire, and my order must be obeyed. But I will do more than give an order to you . . . I will make a last request, *mon ami*. Will you please do as I say? Please . . . '

He was interrupted by another coughing fit. But this spasm soon passed. Garnia continued: 'I am psychic. Does that surprise you? I suppose it does, but it is true. I know when things are going to happen — when they are *supposed* to happen. You two are supposed to be together for a long, long time. Of that I am certain. It is your destiny . . . and any man who turns his back on his destiny is a coward.'

Hayle hesitated no more. He took Garnia's limp hand and pressed it.

Ruth leaned over him. She pressed her lips against his bloodstained mouth.

When she drew back, she did not attempt to wipe the redness away. And Garnia said: 'Hurry, *mes amis*! Please hurry . . . '

They walked out together towards the plane.

Legionnaires were grouped round the tents and near the aircraft. Some were about to remove the remains of Katz, Boroff and Toulez. None of them attempted to stop the two. They had seen them emerge from the lieutenant's tent. Instinct told them what was happening was by authority. And was right.

★　★　★

Garnia made his last great effort.

He rolled out of his bed. On hands and knees, panting like a dog, he crawled towards the tent flap. He clutched the fabric. After a struggle, he managed to pull himself upright. He leaned against the entrance pole.

They entered the plane. He watched them do it. He was smiling. The smile deepened as the engine stuttered into a crescendo of life.

A puzzled sentry came running up. Garnia waved him away. 'It is my order,' he said.

'Your order, *mon officier?* Is it possible?'

Before answering, Garnia raised a shaking finger and pointed to the plane. He said: 'When destiny is aided by courage, then all things are possible.'

'You are ill, *mon officier.* Let me help you back to your bed.'

'Leave me — go!'

Reluctantly, the sentry went.

Garnia stood there, only half upright against the pole, watching the plane manoeuvre for the take-off.

He saw it sweep into the air. It circled over the oasis. A hand waved from one of the side windows. It might have been his. It might have been hers. He did not know. It did not matter. He saw it turn like a homing bird and fly westward.

As he listened to its motors fade, another sound reached his ears. A heavy, throaty noise. Substantial, all-powerful. The noise of the approaching transport plane with soldiers inside it. Fresh soldiers, equipped to renew the law of France.

The great aircraft landed and stopped at the identical spot where the other had been standing. The side door clanged open. A steel ladder was hooked into place. A major of the Legion Airborne Battalion descended it first. He was in full battle order. So were the forty-six men who followed him.

The major spoke to one of Garnia's legionnaires. Then he strode towards the tent. He stopped opposite Garnia.

'You are the officer commanding Post D?'

'I was — there is now no Post D.'

'So I understand. But I believe you have here three deserters and an American citizen. I will require from you a full report for immediate radio transmission to base.'

'There are no deserters. Two are dead. The other a few minutes ago with the American woman . . . left in the plane. It was by my orders.'

The major's face became flaccid. 'Your orders! *Dieu!* But why?'

'They were in love. And it was destiny.'

The major regarded him steadily. Then he asked: 'Are you very ill, lieutenant? I see you have been wounded.'

Garnia managed to shake his head. 'I am ill no longer,' he whispered.

He slid downwards against the tent pole until collapsed on his stomach, the photograph of Marie with him. And it became stained with his blood.

Other titles in the
Linford Mystery Library:

VILLAGE OF FEAR

Noel Lee

After narrowly escaping death on a train, two people find themselves in an eerie deserted village — and make a grisly discovery . . . On a dark and stormy night, locals gather in an inn to tell a frightening tale . . . A writer's country holiday gets off to a bad start when he finds a corpse in his cottage . . . And a death under the dryer at a fashionable hairdressing salon leads to several beneficiaries of the late lady's will falling under suspicion of murder . . .

PUNITIVE ACTION

John Robb

Soldiers of Fort Valeau, a Foreign Legion outpost, discover the mutilated bodies of several men from their overdue relief column, ambushed and massacred by Dylaks. Captain Monclaire's radio report to the garrison at Dini Sadazi results in a promise that more soldiers will be despatched to Valeau, from there to mount punitive action against the offenders. But before the reinforcements arrive, the Dylaks send a message to Monclaire — if he does not surrender, they will attack and conquer the fort . . .

DEATH WALKS SKID ROW

Michael Mallory

Sunset Boulevard, 1975: Two men are speeding home from a party on a night that will haunt them forever. Despite the dangerously wet roads, both passenger and driver are very drunk. Thirty years later on Los Angeles's Skid Row, a homeless man is found dead in an alley. Discovering several disturbing connections, reporter Ramona Rios and a man known on Skid Row only as 'the governor' set out on separate paths to unveil the truth, but are brought together to face a perilous web of power, manipulation and deceit.

ONCE YOU STOP, YOU'RE DEAD

Eaton K. Goldthwaite

The USS *Slocum* is on a routine naval patrol northwest of Bermuda when the SOS crackles over the radio. Cuban National Air's Flight Twelve is ditching in the Atlantic with eighty-nine passengers and five crew aboard. Commander H. P. Perry readies his ship for standard rescue operations — only to discover there's nothing standard about the survivors. Once aboard, they're more demanding than grateful, for most are Russian or Cuban nationals. That's when Commander Perry realizes he's an unwitting pawn in a deadly game, the outcome of which could have grave international repercussions . . .